Flight to Paradise

Also by Gail Newman

Sunshine in the Shadows

Flight to Paradise

Gail Newman

Desert Palm Press

Flight to Paradise

By Gail Newman

©2020 Gail Newman

ISBN (book) 9781948327756
ISBN (epub) 9781948327763
ISBN (pdf) 9781948327770

Desert Palm Press
1961 Main Street, Suite 220
Watsonville, California 95076
www.desertpalmpress.com

Editor: Glenda Poulter
Cover Design: Michele Bordeur - eebooWORX

Printed in the United States of America
First Edition July 2020

Some relationships break your heart. Others feed your soul.

Chapter One

SARA LOOKED AT THE business card in her hand. She flipped it over a few times and stared at the information printed on the front and then the handwritten phone number on the back. Glancing at the clock, she shook her head when she saw it was almost midnight. She sat at her kitchen table, her cell phone and a glass of wine in front of her. She jumped when the cell phone rang.

"I thought you'd never call."

"Hey, hot date. What can I tell you?" Chloe said.

"If it was a hot date, you wouldn't be calling me back until sometime tomorrow." Sara flipped the business card over again.

"That's true. She was nice, but I just wasn't into her. So, your message said you had a strange offer. Did you meet someone at that thing you went to tonight?"

"I did. I met Claire Elliot." Sara smiled to herself at the thought.

"Who?"

"Claire Elliot. Come on, Chloe. I told you about the whole thing. She's an Australian actress who just finished her first movie. She's done theatre here in New York and in London. A moderator interviewed her during the workshop."

"Sorry, Sara. I know you told me, but I think I was texting some chick at the time."

"That's what I love about you, Chloe. I always have your undivided attention," Sara said, shaking her head.

"Hey, now. I'm your best friend and I know you better than anyone."

"What's that got to do with anything?"

"It means that I know when you start talking about something that I'm only slightly interested in, I can concentrate on what I'm doing at the moment and just pay attention to some of what you are saying and still know what's going on."

"Alright. Whatever. Can I just tell you what happened?"

"I promise I'm totally listening."

"What do you think?" she asked after telling Chloe about the evening's events.

"Let me get this straight. You've been asked to become an assistant to an actress I've never heard of, for a position you don't have any experience in."

"That would be correct."

"Sara, as long as I've known you, you've wanted to write. It's your dream. You take classes, you write stuff but don't do anything with it and—"

"Let's not go there. I plan on doing something with it. I just have to finish."

"Again, whatever," Chloe said.

"That's why I'm going to call her in the morning, thank her for the opportunity, but tell her I can't take the job."

"Alright, sounds good. Call me after you do that, and we'll make plans to do something tomorrow night."

"Okay. Talk to you then," Sara said as she swiped the phone to end the call. She continued to sit at the table flipping the business card over and over.

Chapter Two

A YEAR LATER SARA smiled and exchanged hellos with the familiar faces she saw as she walked across the lot of the movie set in Hollywood. Juggling the bag of food, she opened the door to the trailer to find Claire studying her lines.

"Lunch is here," Sara said as she set the bag on the table.

"Thank God. I'm starving and tired of going over this." Claire waved the script in the air as she stood up and stretched her long legs.

"What do you think about today's filming?" Sara began to serve the salad.

"I think," Claire said, looking into the bag, "I think there aren't any cookies."

"I was going to try and save these for later." Sara reached for her handbag and pulled out a package of cookies and dangled them in front of Claire.

"Oh no, you don't." Claire lunged for the bag.

Sara shrieked and pulled the cookies away.

"Now, now. Don't make me have to tackle you. You know I always win." Claire grinned.

Sara noticed the wicked glint in Claire's eyes. "I think I can take you this time." She glared back.

"Okay, guess you'll have to take your chances." Claire pushed a chair towards Sara.

Sara jumped out of the way and ran toward the bathroom. Some movie trailers can be quite spacious, but there isn't a lot of room when you are being chased by a crazed movie star in need of a cookie. She almost made it when Claire caught her, her arms wrapping around Sara's middle as they fell onto the sofa. Claire turned Sara over on her back and pinned her arms down.

"So, my pretty, give me your cookies."

"Well, since I don't seem to have a choice." Sara let the bag drop from her fingers.

For a moment, they continued to stare at each other. Finally, Claire sat up and grabbed the bag.

"You usually put up a better fight," Claire said as she began to open the bag.

Sara laid there for a moment before sitting up next to Claire. "I know. I'm just tired." Sara sighed.

"I'm sorry, darling. That event last night ran longer than we thought." Claire made her way to the front of the trailer. It was the end of awards season and the past week had been full of late nights.

"It wasn't that. After I dropped you off, I stopped to check on Chloe."

"How is she doing?" Claire munched away on a cookie.

Sara went to the table to finish putting out lunch. "She's fine. She flew in to help on a photoshoot and she's not getting along with some of the people. She just wanted to talk some more. She flies back to New York in a couple of days."

Claire joined Sara at the table. "Well, I do hope she'll be alright in the meantime." She patted Sara's hand.

They sat quietly as they ate. When they were done, Claire went back to the sofa and picked up the script.

"By the way, I need you to do something for me."

"What might that be?"

"I need you to get me a cell phone."

"You have a cell phone."

"No, I have a cell phone that you or Abby answers. I need my own cell phone."

"May I ask why you need a cell phone?"

"You may ask, but I won't answer." Claire grinned that wicked grin again.

A knock at the door signaled that Claire was needed on the set.

"So, if you could get it by tomorrow, darling, that would be great." Claire grabbed another cookie and sailed out the door.

Chapter Three

SARA DROVE BACK TO Claire's modest home in the Hollywood Hills in the morning. Claire spent time there only when necessary, and Sara stayed in the guest house. Claire's main home was a brownstone on the upper west side of Manhattan.

"I have your cell phone," Sara said as she entered the spacious living room.

"Excellent." Claire patted the sofa cushion next to her.

"Okay, it's fairly easy to use. Your number is programmed in. I'll just run through some of the functions." Sara removed the phone from its box.

Claire nodded as Sara explained each function. When she was done, Sara placed the phone in Claire's hand.

"This is perfect, darling. Thanks so much."

"And why do you need this cell phone?"

"I have a certain reason." Claire smiled as she continued to look at the phone.

"Does Abby know about this?"

"Abby doesn't need to know everything." Claire got up and slid the phone into a bag sitting on the table.

"Well, it seems to me that she does know everything."

"To you, it might seem that way."

"Well the one thing I definitely know, is that she doesn't like me." Sara laughed.

"Of course she likes you. She's just Abby, that's all. She doesn't tolerate a lot of people. That's why she's such a good agent."

"That's fine. But, I mean, I'm your assistant. I think she could be a little nicer to me."

"Darling, she is nice to you." Claire sat down on the sofa next to her.

"Nice. Okay, let's review some of the nice things she has done. Let's start with when she left me out in the rain at that premiere because, according to her, she forgot I came in the car with her."

"That's easy to explain. There was a lot going on." Claire waved her hand.

"All right, another example. How about when she pushed me out the door after I brought the food in for your holiday party?"

"Again, easily explained. She didn't recognize you and thought you were one of the servers."

"Even if she thought that, why would she push a server out the door?"

"Wait, Abby explained that. She thought you were the paparazzi."

"The best is saved for last. How about when she spilled red wine all over my dress, so I couldn't go to the premiere of your last movie?"

"That was an unfortunate accident." Claire shook her head.

"Accident? She didn't even have a drink until I brought my dress in from the car to change. She went and got the bottle and a glass, proceeded to pour the wine in the glass near the dress, 'tripped' over something imaginary, and then spilled the wine all over the dress while not getting a drop on the rug." Sara crossed her arms across her chest and tilted her head at Claire.

"That might have seemed a little premeditated, but I'm sure she wouldn't do that on purpose."

"Did you know that was the only premiere of yours I have ever been invited to?" Sara waited to hear Claire's answer, but instead of an answer, Claire changed the subject.

"Ah, that reminds me. I would like you to come to London with us."

"What?

"Yes. I need you to come to London with us. We leave Sunday."

"Since when?"

"Since I need you to come. I have some other things going on while we are there that I need your help with."

"Does Abby know you want me along?"

"Yes, I've already told her."

"Will she attempt to push me off the plane?" Sara made a pushing motion.

"Not as long as I'm around." Claire laughed.

"All right, I guess I'll just have to stay near you at all times." Sara shook her head. "What do I need to pack? What will we be doing?"

"We have some scenes for the movie that need to be redone so just your usual wardrobe. Nothing too fancy."

"Good, as I don't have anything too fancy."

"You know what I mean. No evening gowns or anything like that."

"Again, good, as I don't have any evening gowns." Sara laughed.

"What do you mean you don't have any?" Claire gave Sara a puzzled look.

"Why would I have any evening gowns? The only times when I have accompanied you on the red carpet were when Abby was out of town. I wear dark clothes and a tag around my neck, like the other people behind the stars."

"Are you sure?"

"Am I sure I don't have any evening gowns or am I sure of what I do when you're on the red carpet?"

"I guess I hadn't noticed." Claire frowned. "I must do better."

"It doesn't matter. That's what an assistant is for, filling in where I'm needed. I'll just bring what I think will work." Sara stood up. "I'm going to the office to check your emails and do some paperwork. Is there anything else you need right now?"

"No, thank you. I'll just get back to this script."

Sara turned back to look at Claire just as Claire looked up. Their eyes met for a moment before Sara turned and left.

Gail Newman

Chapter Four

THE FLIGHT TO LONDON was calm and relaxing, especially since Sara was in first class. She expected to be relegated to the cargo area with Abby along. She got a little sleep, but not before checking to see if Abby was asleep first. *Better safe than sorry.* She chuckled to herself.

They arrived at The Parker on the Thames, Claire's favorite London hotel. From moment Claire stepped out of the car the hotel staff couldn't have done more for her. She was gracious and remembered staff members' names.

Sara tipped the bellman when they arrived at the suite. "How do you do that?" she asked as she joined Claire in the room.

"Do what darling?" Claire was pulling off her scarf.

"You remember people's names and make them feel at ease."

"It's called being kind. Can't let fame go to your head, my darling. We all have to start somewhere."

Sara took some of the bags into the bedroom.

"What are my engagements for this evening?" Claire stood at the window when Sara returned to the living room for the rest of the bags.

"You have dinner with Todd this evening. Tomorrow you go straight to the studio to start on your scenes. Depending on how long that takes, you also need to complete any voice overs before we leave," Abby said as she sat on the sofa and spread a handful of papers she pulled from her bag on the low table in front of her.

"I want to host a dinner for Todd's new film," Claire said.

"Yes, I have that."

"Also, please make sure I have nothing planned for Friday evening after seven."

Abby opened her date book. "I've blocked out anything after six to allow you time to get ready."

"Perfect, darling. Thanks." Claire smiled at Abby.

"I've hung your clothes in the closet. Do you need me to help you with anything else?" Sara asked.

"No thanks, darling. I'm just going to take a quick shower and freshen up."

Sara found herself alone with Abby in the living room. *Might as well get a reading on how she feels about me today.* She took a deep breath. "Is there anything special I need to be aware of for Claire while we're here?"

"Just a few things. We'll be out tonight, so unless she says something before we go, you're free for the evening. She'll need you to go with her to the studio each day to do the usual, fetch lunch, things like that. Since we have no idea what time she'll finish each day, you'll need to be on call when you return to the hotel for whatever she may decide to do. Friday evening you may make yourself scarce."

"I'm sorry?"

"She has plans in place that won't involve you in any way. Once you get back from the studio you can have the evening off and not plan on seeing her."

Sara was about to comment when Claire called for Abby from the bedroom.

"Coming." Abby got up and brushed past Sara.

Sara stood there for a few minutes looking toward the bedroom before sitting on the sofa. *Guess at some point I'll find out what that was all about.*

A few minutes later Claire came back with Abby following behind her.

"All right, we are off." Claire looked stunning in a dark blue pantsuit.

Sara jumped up from the sofa. "Do you need anything?"

Claire stopped and thought for a moment. "No, darling. I won't be late as I'm exhausted. We're just having a quick dinner with Todd. Why don't you get something to eat and get some sleep? I'll need you around eight tomorrow morning to get us a little breakfast before the car comes at nine."

"I'll be ready."

"Great. Thanks, darling. See you in the morning," Claire called as she and Abby went out the door.

Sara went down the hall to her own room. She sat on the bed and took off her shoes before checking the room service menu. It didn't take long for room service to bring her a sandwich and a bowl of soup. She fell asleep almost as soon as she finished eating.

Chapter Five

PROMPTLY AT EIGHT O'CLOCK the next morning, Sara tapped on Claire's door. Claire opened it wearing a robe with a towel on her head, fresh from the shower.

"Looks like someone got up early." Sara looked around the living room which was littered with pages from Claire's script.

"I did. I thought I would get a good night's sleep, but my eyes popped wide open this morning. Probably just nerves."

"Nerves? Are you nervous?"

Claire took the towel off her head and started drying her hair with it. "Yes, I suppose I am a little." She smiled at Sara.

"I never think of you as getting the nervous type."

"Well, now you know a little secret of mine." Clair threw the towel at Sara. "Now, while I get dressed, please order up some tea, eggs, and toast, and whatever you might like, and we'll get a start on the day."

"Hey, you forgot something." Sara threw the towel back at Claire as she picked up the phone.

They chatted lightly as they ate. When they finished, Sara gathered up a bag of the items Claire thought she might need for the day. Downstairs a waiting car took them to the studio. It was the usual set up—a sound stage for filming the scenes and trailers for the actors to use for changing and resting between scenes. Sara carried the bag to their assigned trailer and Claire followed her.

"Our home away from home." Claire looked around. "Not as nice as the one I had last time I was here."

Sara thought back to that time. Claire had been dating one of her co-stars, Michael Hemsworth, at the time. Sara hadn't relished the awkward moments when she arrived in the morning to find he had spent the night. Even though she was not surprised that Claire was sleeping with Michael, it wasn't an image Sara wanted. The relationship ended badly with Claire getting hurt. The plan was for Michael to return to the states with Claire and for them to attend the premieres together as a couple. An excuse kept him in London and, right before the New

York premiere, he broke the news to Claire that he was seeing someone else. Claire had to deal with being on the red carpet with him smiling and doing interviews about what a great costar he had been while all the time wanting to knee him in the balls. At least that was what she told Sara she wanted to do.

"No need to think about that." Sara smiled.

"No, no reason at all." Claire returned the smile. "Let's get me into this outfit and off to make-up. Hopefully we won't have too long a day."

Sara lifted the dress off the hanger as she asked, "Is Abby joining you on the set today?"

"Yes. A little later. She's arranging interviews which I don't know how I'll have time to do."

"I understand you have plans for Friday evening?" Sara placed the dress over Claire's head.

"I do."

"You won't need me for anything?"

"No, I won't. You can make plans to go sightseeing or whatever you want to do." Claire finished adjusting the dress as Sara handed her the coat that went with it.

"I was just making sure since Abby mentioned it last night."

"Did she now?"

"Yes. She basically said to make myself scarce."

"I think that's a little much, but yes, I have plans for the evening that I won't need any help with. Really, darling, we must get me off to make-up." Claire picked up the matching gloves and moved toward the door while Sara grabbed the bag and followed her.

***

"Help me get out of this." Claire was tugging at the dress stuck around her shoulders.

"Hold still." Sara dropped the bag she was holding to the floor of the trailer and rushed to help her.

It was the second day of shooting and the day had not gone well. Lighting was off and there were problems with sound. All around, it was not a good day.

"There," Sara said as she finally got the dress over Claire's head

Once free, Claire worked to remove her jewelry. "What a piss poor day. God, I need a drink."

"As soon as we get you changed and ready to go, I'm sure there will be enough time to get you a drink before your interview."

"Honestly, I don't care if it's during the interview, I just need a drink."

Sara started to say something when Claire's cell phone rang from inside her handbag. They looked at each other and then at the bag. Claire pulled the phone out and, turning away from Sara, answered it.

Sara, trying to be as nonchalant as possible, tried to hear the other voice.

"Yes, darling, I know. I'm looking forward to seeing you as well. Yes, I think we can. Aren't you the naughty one?" Claire glanced over her shoulder at Sara.

Sara resumed putting the day's costumes away.

"I have to run. Can we finish this later? Great. Bye for now." Claire swiped the phone to end the call and put it back in her bag. "That's that. I'll just change and we can be off. Be a darling and hand me my dress."

Okay. I guess we aren't going to talk about that and, if she doesn't say anything, I'm certainly not going to ask. "Which shoes did you want?" Sara held up two pairs for Claire to decide between.

"I think the red, don't you?"

"Absolutely."

They moved toward each other at the same time and almost knocked each other over. Claire grabbed Sara and steadied her as Sara took hold of Claire's arm.

"That was close," Claire said.

"Yes." Sara was still holding on.

"You okay?"

"Yes."

Claire rubbed Sara's arm as she let her go. "Good. Can't lose you now." Claire took the shoes from Sara's hand and sat down to put them on.

"Alright, I think I'm ready. Let me do a quick check on my hair and make-up and I think we should be off. Are you all set?"

"I think so." Sara picked up the bag she carried for Claire plus her own bag and coat.

"Perfect. Let's go." Claire smiled and looked at Sara. "Do I need to get you a drink as well?"

Sara shook her head. "I think I'll be fine, thanks." One thing she knew for sure was there would be a large martini in her near future.

Gail Newman

Chapter Six

THE NEXT THREE DAYS were a blur spent running between the studio and interviews. Thursday evening Claire hosted a dinner at a small restaurant for her friend Todd Holden, whose first movie as a director was being screened later that night. Both Sara and Abby, as well as some of Todd's friends, were invited.

People were already gathered in the bar area as they arrived. Sara joined them and relaxed as she chatted with some of the people standing near her. As she sipped her wine and looked around, she met the gaze of a woman sitting at the bar. Sara smiled and turned away. The next thing she knew, the woman was standing in front of her.

"Hi there. I'm Anne Hastings."

Sara noticed that Anne was about her height with long, auburn hair, green eyes, and an English accent. "I'm Sara Burton."

"It's nice to meet you, Sara," Anne said as she extended her hand.

"Nice to meet you too." Sara politely shook her hand.

"Are you with the media?"

"No, I'm not." Sara was not in the habit of telling people she was Claire's assistant.

"Just a fan of Todd's?"

"Yes."

"I am too." Anne sipped her drink through a tiny black straw. "I work as a costume designer and I dressed him for some of his films. We became friends so I'm here to support him."

"Oh, that's great."

"Yes, I'm so hoping he has great success as a director. Are you here with someone?"

"Here with someone?" Sara repeated.

"You know...on a date."

"No." Sara chuckled. "No, I'm sort of working."

"How does one 'sort of work' while holding a glass of wine? Oh, I know, I bet you work for someone here. Is it someone famous?" Anne scanned the crowd.

"No, not really." Sara began to feel a little uncomfortable.

"Don't suppose you'd like to go somewhere later and chat?" Anne touched Sara's arm.

"Um, I really don't think I can." *Quick, think of something to get out of this.*

"There you are. Can I grab you to go over a few things?" Abby said as she appeared next to Sara.

"Of course, you can. Sorry, Anne. It was nice to meet you."

Abby took Sara's elbow and started to lead her away. When they were far enough away, Abby let go of her.

"Thanks. I wasn't sure how to get out of that," Sara said.

"No need to thank me. I just wanted to remind you to make yourself scarce tomorrow night."

Yes. I know. You've told me enough times. "Oh, no problem. I'm sure I can find something to do."

"Good," Abby said as she disappeared into the crowd.

Dinner was announced and people started filing into the dining room. While making sure she avoided Anne as she made her way into the room, Sara saw Claire and Abby whispering to one another.

Wonder what that's all about?

Chapter Seven

BY FIVE O'CLOCK FRIDAY evening Claire and Sara were back in the trailer. The disasters from earlier in the week had been resolved and things had gone better since then.

"Let's just pack things up so we can get back to the hotel." Claire handed the day's costume to Sara.

"Yes, we don't want you to be late for your evening." Sara had been trying to think of a way to bring the subject up all day. It bothered her that she didn't know what Claire's plans were.

"You should have a nice relaxing evening for yourself." Claire sat on the edge of a chair pulling off her stockings. "Perhaps you and Abby could have dinner together."

"Funny. I don't think that's an option." *So, Abby is not involved in these plans. Maybe I can figure this out without asking.* Sara's mind was racing. "Do you need me to come around later?" Sara began to hang up the clothes.

"No."

"What time tomorrow morning should I check-in?"

"Um." Claire got up and placed the stockings in a small hamper. "How about I call your room or your cell when I'm up and about?"

"Okay."

Claire pulled on some jeans and a sweater. "Are you ready?"

"Yes, I think I have everything." Sara looked around to make sure.

They were both quiet in the car until Claire broke the silence. "Perhaps you could contact the girl you were chatting with last night."

"Girl? What girl?"

Claire smiled at her. "The lovely young redhead from the restaurant."

"Oh, Anne. You mean Anne." Sara nodded as she thought back to the previous evening.

"You didn't know her?"

"No. Actually, she's a friend of Todd's. She said she started as his dresser or something on his films and they became friends."

"And?"

"And what?"

"She seemed quite interested in you," Claire was looking out the car window.

"I guess. I mean, she did ask me if I wanted to go somewhere and chat."

"So, she was interested?"

"I'm not sure what she was interested in, but I do know I was not."

"Not your type?"

"Not my type and not at work." Sara laughed.

Claire ran her hand through her hair. "What is your type? I don't think I know." Claire looked away from the passing view and turned to Sara.

"That would be because it's been a while since I had a type."

"No, seriously." Claire touched Sara's arm. "Who was the last girl you dated?"

"Why are we discussing this?" *I don't want to talk about it.*

"Because that girl wanted to take you home last night."

"Now wait a minute. We certainly weren't going down that road and, if she did, she was going alone."

Claire put her finger to her lips. "What was her name? She was cute and had blonde hair. Prissy or Patty or something like that."

"Prissy, what is that? Some sort of Australian name?"

"Pammy or Tammy?"

Finally, Sara couldn't take it anymore. "Her name was Lynne. Where you were going with those other names, I don't know."

"That's right, Lynne." Claire slapped her hand on her thigh. "Whatever happened to her?"

Sara shook her head. "Why are we talking about this?"

"Because of last evening," Claire answered.

"We were together for a little while and I felt it wasn't going anywhere."

"How do you mean?"

"I think your feelings should grow the longer you see someone if it's going to be something. My feelings weren't going anywhere."

"Maybe you didn't give it enough time."

"Look, Claire. I've only dated a few men and even fewer women, but I do know how I want to feel about someone. I think that I can tell whether or not something is going to work."

"How many of each did you date?"

Sara put her hands over her face. "Why, oh why, are we talking about this?"

"Because of last night."

Claire pulled Sara's hands away from her face and held them for a minute.

Sara looked down at their hands. "I had a high school boyfriend, one in college, and then Lynne."

"Were you intimate with all of them?" Claire whispered.

"Only the college guy and Lynne."

"May I ask a question? I don't think we've ever talked about this. When did you realize you liked women?"

"Growing up I had girl crushes but then boys came into the picture. It wasn't until I met Lynne, and she was a lesbian, that I found out that girl crushes could become relationships. I just connect better with women."

Tears welled up in Sara's eyes as the car pulled in front of the hotel.

"My darling, what's wrong?" Claire asked as she took hold of Sara's hand.

"It's nothing Claire." Sara quickly wiping the tears from her eyes.

"Surely, it's something for you to be upset and, if I've upset you by asking you about this, I'm so very sorry. I want you to know that I am your friend. You know that, don't you?"

"Yes Claire. But foremost you are my boss, and sometimes being honest with you about my personal life is just a little strange."

"Honesty. Yes, there is a lot to be said about that." Claire lowered her eyes and turned slightly.

"Really Claire, I'm alright. I probably just need a good night's sleep."

"Might do us both some good." Claire patted Sara's hands as she took hers away.

Claire tapped on the window that was between them and the driver. A moment later, the door opened and the doorman helped Claire from the car. Sara collected herself, accepted the doorman's assistance, and followed Claire inside.

"I'll see you tomorrow," Claire said as they walked out of the elevator.

"Goodnight, Claire." Sara turned in the direction of her room.

Gail Newman

Chapter Eight

SARA WOKE THE NEXT morning and looked at the clock on the nightstand. It was nine o'clock. She turned on her back, looked at the ceiling, and thought of the previous evening. Since she couldn't sleep after her conversation with Claire, she had gone for a walk.

As she walked up and down the streets near the hotel, she found a small pub that she might have passed by any other time. The small front window had a candle lit in it and Sara felt it was calling her. Inside she found a table for two at the window and sat down. A server came around and introduced herself as Petula. She went through the list of specials. Sara hadn't really thought about eating since she was still a little upset.

"I'd rather just have a glass of red wine."

"Ah, so you need a glass of wine. Lovers quarrel?" Petula handed Sara a menu.

"No. Why would you think that?"

"Well, you look a little upset and you're alone."

Wow, this woman is nosey. "I could be waiting for someone."

"If you were, you would have said that from the start."

"I'm not sure about that, but yes, I am alone, and no, there wasn't a lover's quarrel."

"But someone has upset you?"

"Yes, but it might just be me. I'm not sure."

"I think that calls for a plate of Bangers and Mash." Petula put her finger to her lips and looked up as if waiting for an answer from above.

"Any reason in particular you would recommend that?" Sara opened the menu, a little stunned by Petula's suggestion.

"It's a hearty meal and I think you need something hearty. But I'll get your wine first, then you can decide." Petula walked off toward the bar.

Sara sat looking at the menu and, after a few moments, realized she wasn't paying any attention to it. She glanced around the restaurant. Other people had filtered in while she was talking with

Petula—couples at tables and small groups of friends at the bar. Eyeing each couple, she tried to figure out which ones were on a date or married. Two couples caught her attention. One couple, probably around her age, were excitedly chatting back and forth. The other, an older couple, sat quietly, he drinking his beer, and she her martini. Occasionally, one would make a comment that the other acknowledged with a word or nod, but nothing more than that.

What's the difference? Was the younger couple newly in love and making their life plans and the older couple so set and content with each other that they didn't have much to say to one another? The older couple's seeming lack of interest in each other bothered her. She was saved from doing a self-analysis by Petula returning with her wine.

"So, love, have you decided?" Petula placed the glass on the table.

"I...I think I still need a minute." Sara struggled to get the words out.

"Take your time. I'll keep the wine coming."

"No, I'd better not. Too much wine will just put me over the edge." *Why would I say that to a stranger?*

Petula pulled the other chair out and sat down. "There, there, love. Nothing can ever be that bad that it can't be fixed. Why don't you tell me what's going on?"

"But I don't even know you."

"Ah, but sometimes that's the best thing." Petula smiled.

Sara wrapped her hands around the glass. "I can't even explain it."

"Sure, you can. You just have to think about it for a moment."

Without thinking, Sara said the first thing that came to her mind, "I feel invisible."

"There you go. Now, tell me why."

"I don't feel like anyone pays any attention to me. Like my boss and the other woman who works for her. I'm there and I do things, really personal things for her, but it's like I just appear to them when I'm needed."

"Well, you know how you can fix that, don't you?" Petula's smile grew wide. "You have to make sure you're not invisible to yourself."

"I don't understand." Sara took a sip of her wine.

"You have to see yourself as you want others to see you. If you want them to see you as bold and confident, then you must see yourself that way. If they don't see you that's because you're making yourself invisible. You have to see yourself the way you want people to see you." Petula grabbed Sara's hand.

"Hey, this food's not gonna serve itself," a man bellowed from the kitchen.

"I'm coming," Petula bellowed back at him as she got up from the table.

"Now, I'm going to get you some Bangers and Mash. I will bring you one more glass of wine when you're ready, and while I do that, you are going to think about what I said."

"I will." Sara gave her a weak smile.

"Work on that smile. I know you can do better." Petula pinched one of Sara's cheeks and went to the kitchen.

Sara sat there for a moment before looking around. The young couple now sat quietly, looking everywhere but at each other, and the older couple were now holding hands across the table and chatting away. *Guess I have a lot to think about.*

Gail Newman

Chapter Nine

SARA'S CELL PHONE RANG at eleven o'clock as she sat looking down at the river from the window.

"Good morning, darling. I'm up and about. Can you come to my room?" Claire asked.

"I'll be right there."

Claire opened the door to Sara's soft knock. She was wearing white silk pajamas with a teal silk robe over them.

Does Claire always look this beautiful when she wakes up?

"So, darling, how are you this morning?" Claire poured tea from a silver teapot into a cup. She handed the cup to Sara and stood directly in front of her.

"I'm fine, thank you."

Claire tilted her head at Sara. "Are you sure? I don't know why but you seem a little off this morning. Are you feeling alright?"

"Yes, I'm fine. How are you?"

"I'm wonderful but worried about you."

Sara walked to the table and dropped a cube of sugar and a dash of milk into her teacup.

"I forget you like it like that." Claire walked to a chair nearby and sat down.

"Not surprising." Sara sat facing Claire.

Claire put down her teacup and folded her arms across her chest. "What exactly is that supposed to mean?"

Sara caught herself. *No reason to get into anything with Claire when I'm not sure why I'm upset.* "I'm sorry, Claire. I didn't sleep well last night."

Claire seemed to relax. "I'm sorry, darling. Do we need to get you something to help?"

"No, I don't think so. I'm sure I'll be able to work it all out."

"Work out what?"

"Sorry, bad choice of words. I mean, I'm sure the sleep thing will work itself out. It was probably something I ate last night."

"Oh. So, what did you do last night?" Claire resumed drinking her tea.

"I walked around for a while, and then had dinner in this great little pub I found. I almost passed it by."

"Really? Where?"

"I didn't want to go too far from the hotel, so I walked out the front door, turned right, and walked down a few blocks. Do you know it?"

"It sounds like somewhere I might have been. But never mind that," Claire said with a wave of her hand.

Okay, whatever. Guess I'll change the subject. "How was your evening?"

Claire put the teacup down and ran her fingers through her hair. "It was lovely, thank you."

"I'm glad."

They were both quiet. Sara was lost in her thoughts.

"Did you have breakfast?" Claire asked.

"I woke up about nine and had a croissant."

"I need to get ready. The car will be here in an hour to take us to the studio." Claire finished her tea and got up. "Be a darling and put the script in the bag. We don't need to take anything else. I'm hoping we can finish up today and go back to New York tomorrow."

"Really?" Sara was surprised by this news. "I thought you had a few more days of shooting."

"Apparently some editing has been done and the director thinks they might have all they'll need. I'll go and change."

***

Claire came back into the room and stood in front of Sara. She ever so gently brushed Sara's bangs with her finger. "Are you sure you're alright?" She looked Sara square in the eye as if searching for the real answer.

Sara took a deep breath. "I'm fine."

"I'll trust you're telling me the truth then." Claire smiled. "Oh, now what have I done with my phone? I'll be right back." She turned and walked towards the bedroom.

Sara took another deep breath and looked around the room. Something red under a sofa cushion caught her eye. She walked over to see what it was. Lifting the cushion, she pulled it out. She was shocked to find a woman's lacy bra dangling from her fingers.

26

"What the…?" she said out loud. Since she purchased most of Claire's intimate apparel, Sara was pretty sure it didn't belong to Claire. *But who, then*? She hadn't wanted to think about the mysterious evening, but this brought it to a new level of suspicion.

"Sara, darling, don't forget my handbag," Claire called from the bedroom.

Startled, Sara dropped the bra on the floor. Panicked that Claire would return to the living room, she picked the bra up and stuck it behind a sofa pillow. After a moment she decided she wanted answers. She picked the bra up with one finger and walked toward the bedroom.

"Ah, Claire?"

Sara stuck her arm inside the door, dangling the bra. "Is this yours?"

The bra disappeared from her finger. "That was sent over by a designer and it must have fallen out of the box. It's not my style. I'm about ready. Are you ready to go?"

Sara backed into the living room smiling as she said, "Yes. I'm ready when you are." *I guess, just as you have to trust me, I'll have to trust that you are telling me the truth. Not.*

Gail Newman

Chapter Ten

THEY FLEW BACK TO New York on Sunday. Not a word was spoken about the bra. In fact, very few words were spoken. Claire and Abby were meeting friends for dinner, so the car dropped Sara off at her apartment before taking them to the restaurant. Sara wanted to say something to Claire—what, she didn't know—but things felt strange and she didn't like it. All she was able to do was say she would see her the next morning.

As the car pulled away from the curb, Sara stood and watched until it disappeared into the city traffic. She finally tugged her luggage onto the elevator and up to her fourth-floor apartment. Once inside, she collapsed into the chair next to the window. Looking out at the grey skies, she felt lost and alone. When the phone rang, she jumped to grab it without looking. *It must be Claire.*

"Hello?"

"Hey, there's my best friend. So glad you're back," Chloe said.

"Hey."

"What's wrong?"

Sara started to cry. "I don't know, I'm just...I'm just...I don't know."

"I'll be there in five."

Before she knew it, Chloe was there holding her as she cried. Chloe kept telling her to get it out. When she was able, Sara stopped crying. She wiped her eyes, blew her nose, and started to talk.

"Why am I doing this? Why am I working for someone who doesn't appreciate me, and won't tell me what's going on?"

"Hold on there. What are you talking about? Claire has always been good to you."

"Why aren't I writing screenplays? Why aren't I dating? Why am I always doing things for her?"

"Ah, because that's your job. Seriously, what has you all fired up?"

"Because I realized I'm invisible to Claire and Abby."

"Now wait a minute, don't count Abby in this. We know how that woman feels about you."

"That's another thing. Why does she feel that way about me?" Sara got up, went to the kitchen, and brought back a bottle of wine and two glasses. "I went to a pub one night while we were in London. I met this server named Petula, and out of nowhere, she's telling me things about myself and what I need to do for myself. It was the weirdest thing."

"Sounds like I need to go there with you. Maybe she can help me." Chloe chuckled.

"Then there's this thing with Claire."

"What thing with Claire?"

"Before we left for London, she wanted her own cell phone that neither Abby nor I would have access to."

"Why is that weird?"

"Because one of us always handles her calls. But that's not all of it. As soon as we got to London, I was told by Abby to make myself scarce Friday night as Claire had plans and I wouldn't be needed."

"Was that the night you met Petula?"

"Yes and the next morning Claire didn't call until eleven. When I went to her room, she was all dreamy and looked beautiful in this lounging outfit."

"What's wrong with that?"

"I don't know. Nothing, I guess. But when I started to get things ready to leave for the set, I saw something red under the sofa cushion. When I pulled it out, it was a red bra." Sara nodded.

"Again, what's wrong with that?"

"It wasn't something Claire would wear or owns as far as I know."

"Okay, I'm no detective here." Chloe refilled their wine glasses. "But it doesn't seem too hard to figure out that Claire is seeing someone."

"What? No. For a brief moment I thought that, but no."

"Wow, Sara, come on. The cell phone, make yourself scarce, the red bra. Obviously she's seeing some guy."

"But I usually know who she's seeing."

"Maybe he's married or something and they don't want it to get out."

"You think? I wouldn't say anything."

"Claire knows that, but this guy doesn't. He's probably asking her to keep this really low. Best thing you can do is follow Claire's lead. Don't push. She'll come around. At some point she's going to have to tell you something."

Sara felt better. The more she thought about it the better she felt.

"You're probably right. Claire knows she can trust me, but she must be in a position right now where she can't say anything."

"I'm sure that's what it is." Chloe hugged Sara.

"In the meantime." Sara held her glass up. "Here's to me, because I'm going to start looking out for myself. I'm going to work on the screenplay I've started and put down so many times and this time I'm going to finish it. Never know when Claire might decide I'm not needed anymore."

Chloe held up her glass. "I don't know about Claire deciding that, but you never know about Abby."

"To protecting myself," Sara said.

"To protecting yourself." Chloe smiled as they clicked their glasses together.

Gail Newman

Chapter Eleven

SARA ARRIVED AT CLAIRE'S townhouse Monday morning. Once inside, she hung up her coat and checked to see what had been left on her desk while she was away. The housekeeper had stacked the mail in a neat pile on the corner of the desk. Sara decided to deal with the mail later and made her way up the stairs.

Sara stood behind one of the chairs in the second floor living room and ran her hand over the top of it. She loved this house. Her little one-bedroom apartment couldn't compare with it. The house was quiet, so she went back to the staircase and looked up the stairs to the third floor where the bedrooms were located. Normally she would have gone up, but she hesitated since she didn't know if Claire had someone with her.

Clearing her throat, she called, "Claire?" Nothing. Sara went up a few steps and called again. "Claire?"

Claire looked over the banister from the floor above. "Good heavens, darling, what are you doing? Just come up."

Sara was caught off guard and tripped on the next step. She caught herself before she fell.

Claire rounded the staircase and stood at the top. "Are you alright?"

"Yes, I'm fine. I guess my balance is still off from the flight." Sara continued up the stairs as Claire waited for her.

"Why don't we get you into a chair?" Claire met her at the top of the steps, took her by the arm, and led her into her bedroom. The large bedroom overlooked the backyard patio. It also had a comfortable sitting area in front of the fireplace. Claire made sure Sara was safely in a chair and pulled another close to her. "Are you sure you're alright?"

"Of course. I'm just still thrown off from the trip. I'm not as well traveled as you."

"Is that all it is?"

"Yes. Why wouldn't it be?" Sara raised her eyebrows.

"You seem a little off recently and I've been worried about you. You would tell me if something was wrong, wouldn't you?" Claire asked as she took Sara's hand.

"Yes, I would. Really I'm fine. You're alright too, aren't you?"

"Yes. Why would you think I wasn't?"

"Because of the trip, finishing the movie. Is there anything I can help you with?"

Claire squeezed Sara's hand as she let it go. "No. Everything is just fine."

"Good. So, we're both fine." Sara stood up. "I'll go back down to the office and sort through the mail. Is Abby coming in today?"

"Yes, a little later. Once she arrives, we'll go over the plans for the week. I'll tell you now that I have plans for Thursday evening, so I'll be unavailable after seven o'clock. Of course, Abby can contact me if I'm needed."

"Alright, no problem. Do you need anything now?"

"No. Mrs. Hanson will be in at ten o'clock. I told her to come in late in case I slept in."

"I guess I'll see you later."

Sara returned to the office and started going through the mail. *Hmm, another evening out with the mystery man. Who could it be? Maybe Chloe is right. Maybe it is some married guy sneaking around. Perhaps between now and Thursday I can pick up some clues who it might be.*

Chapter Twelve

THE NEXT FEW DAYS were business as usual. Sara didn't pick up any hints on who the mystery man might be. Thursday afternoon, as she was going up the stairs to have Claire sign some paperwork, she met Abby on her way down.

"Are you leaving?" Sara asked.

"Yes. Did you need something?"

"I have some paperwork on the corner of my desk I was going to give to you on your way out. Would you like to take it with you, or should I give it to you tomorrow?"

"I'll take it on my way out." Abby continued down the stairs. "Oh and, Sara."

Sara stopped at the top of the stairs. "Yes."

"Remember that Claire is unavailable this evening."

"Yes, I know."

Sara watched as Abby went into the office, came out with the paperwork, and left. *Now that she's gone I'll see what Claire has to say, if anything.* Sara made her way to the living room. Claire sat on the sofa thumbing through a home remodel magazine.

"What do you think, darling? Should I remodel this place to be more modern?"

Sara stood next to her to look at the picture. "No, you can't do that here. This is perfect."

"You think?" Claire looked around.

"Are you kidding? This house was built in the 1930s and you have done so much to try and keep its charm. Why would you want to change it?"

"I don't want to change everything, but the furniture and the appliances in these pictures would make it seem cleaner and sleeker."

"Oh my God, Claire, that's not how this house should be." Tears started to well in Sara's eyes, but she controlled herself. "I'm sorry, Claire. It's your house. You can certainly do with it what you want."

"I don't know. You had a strong reaction to the idea."

"No, no. I don't handle change well and when I feel things are perfect, I think they should stay that way." Sara quickly covered. *Calm down, it's not your house. But if it were, I would never think of changing it.*

"So, what do you have for me?" Claire asked as she closed the magazine.

Sara sat down next to her and put the paperwork on the coffee table in front of them. "A few things to sign. I'd also like to get your schedule for next week. I have some appointments we need to schedule for you."

"I have a general idea of what my schedule is, and what I don't know, Abby can tell you."

"I know you have plans for this evening. Should I arrive at my usual time tomorrow?" *Let's see how she answers this.*

"Yes, that's fine."

"Anything in particular I need to know about tomorrow?"

"No."

Well, this is going nowhere fast. "Anything you need me to do for tomorrow before I leave?"

Claire got up and walked to the dining room. She opened the liquor cabinet and pulled out a bottle of scotch whiskey. She placed two ice cubes in a glass and poured the whiskey over them. "Would you like something?"

"No, thanks." *Wow. I've never seen Claire drink whiskey, let alone drink in the afternoon. Should I say something? As a friend, I probably should. As her assistant...yup, don't think I'll comment on this.* "Look at the time. I'm sure you need to get ready. I'll just go and finish up in the office."

Claire took a sip of the drink and turned toward Sara. "That's fine. I'll see you tomorrow."

"See you tomorrow." Sara stayed in the office for another half an hour. When she was about to leave, she called Chloe. "Hey, it's me. Are you doing anything this evening?"

"No. What's up?"

"Claire has another mysterious date this evening. Want to join me on the case?"

"Sounds like fun. Where should I meet you?"

"It's about five now and her plans are for seven. She'll have to leave at some point before then. I'll go over to Henry's. Meet me there."

"On my way."

Henry's was a pub down the street from Claire's brownstone. Sara knew if they positioned themselves right, they would be able to see Claire leave.

Sara pulled on her coat and called Claire on the intercom. "Claire, I'm leaving."

"That's fine, darling. Have a good evening."

"Thanks. You too."

Sara walked down the street to Henry's and sat at the first table by the window. She checked to make sure nothing blocked the view. She ordered a glass of wine while she waited for Chloe, who arrived soon after.

Chloe kissed Sara on the cheek before she sat down. "What's the plan?" Chloe asked after giving the waiter her drink order.

"Follow her," Sara whispered as she leaned toward Chloe.

"Really?"

Sara thought about it for a minute and then waved her hand. "This is probably ridiculous. What difference does it make what she's doing? If she wanted me to know, I'd know. Let's just forget about it and enjoy our drinks."

"Oh, no you don't. You got me down here, so if you don't follow her, I will." Chloe shook her head.

"You can't follow her." Sara's voice raised as panic set in.

"Why not?"

"Suppose she catches you?" Sara lowered her voice and pointed at her.

"How would she catch me? If she goes someplace that it wouldn't make sense for me to be, I won't go in."

"That does sound like a good plan. We could follow from a distance just to get an idea of where she goes." Sara nodded.

"Now you're talking."

"Okay, we'll sit here until she comes out." Sara took a sip of her drink.

"How will she get where she's going?" Chloe asked.

Sara saw a black town car pull up in front of the brownstone and almost spat her drink out. "The car's there."

Chloe spun around in her seat. "Now we know she got car service. How are we going to follow her?"

"Good question." Sara jumped up. "You hail a cab and I'll pay the bill. Or I'll hail the cab while you pay but we have to get in the cab before she comes out of the house."

"What if the car service is early? Then we'll be sitting in a cab with the meter running."

"Good point. Okay, we pay the bill, go look for a cab, and wait to hop in when we need to." Sara looked for the waiter.

"Then it would be just our luck that someone else takes the cab before we do. Let's remain calm. Here comes our waiter. Give him some cash and let's go."

Sara looked at the bill, left the cash, and in a second they were on the street looking for a cab. She looked toward the brownstone and saw Claire coming out the door and walking toward the car. "There she is."

Chloe began waving frantically at every passing cab. Finally, one pulled over. They almost knocked each other over trying to get in. Sara looked out the back window and saw the town car coming towards them. She turned to the driver as the town car was passing them.

"Sir, maybe you have or haven't heard this before, but follow that car."

"Whatever you say, lady," the cab driver said as he took off after the town car.

Settling in, Sara and Chloe looked at each other and started to laugh. "You know, I was just starting to think about how boring my life was lately." Chloe wiped tears from her eyes.

"You? I'm the one that's invisible."

"Alright, so tonight we won't be boring or invisible. We're going to be adventurous." Chloe stuck out her hand.

Sara shook it. "To adventurous. We shall see what the night brings."

They sat back in the cab waiting to see where it took them.

***

After what seemed to be an eternity of blurred buildings whizzing by, the cab finally came to a halt. Sara checked to be sure the town car was still in front of them as she tried to make sense of where they were.

The driver of the town car got out, opened the back door, and clasped the outstretched hand of his passenger. Sara gasped. A stunning Claire, wearing a long red cape, emerged from the car. When Claire turned to address the driver, Sara could see she wore the spectacular black beaded dress she bought the last time they were in Los Angeles. Claire turned and entered the building.

"Chloe, where are we?" Sara asked.

"At the Plum Room. What do you want to do?"

"I don't know. I've never been here. I don't know what the layout is."

"You stay here." Chloe opened the cab door. "I'll go in and scope it out."

"What if she sees you?"

"Don't worry. I'll come up with something." Chloe got out of the cab and made her way to the door. After carefully looking inside, she went in.

Sara tapped her foot as she waited. After almost five minutes Chloe emerged from the building and got in the cab. "Well?"

Chloe looked at her. "She's not in there."

"What? What do you mean she's not in there?"

"Sara, I looked everywhere. I checked the bar, the tables. She's not in there."

"She has to be. We saw her go inside." Sara leaned over Chloe to look at the building.

"I'm telling you she's not in there," Chloe said.

"Maybe she was in the bathroom."

"I thought about that and I watched two women go in and come out. Then I went in. There's only one stall. Unless she was hiding in the cabinet while the other women came in and out, she wasn't in there."

"What the fuck?" Sara slumped back in the seat.

"It goes through to the hotel," the cabbie said.

"I'm sorry, what?" Sara asked.

The driver turned to look at them. "The restaurant opens into the hotel lobby. A lot of famous people use this entrance so they aren't seen."

"So, you mean—"

"The main hotel entrance is around the block, so they go through this entrance and into the hotel. Meter's still running, ladies. What do you want to do?" He turned back to the steering wheel.

"What the fuck?" Sara said again.

"She went in this entrance, walked through, and is in the hotel." Chloe tapped her chin with her finger. "Very interesting. What do you want to do?"

"I have no idea." Sara shook her head.

"Let's walk through and see if we find her."

"We can't do that." Sara put her hand up.

"Why not?"

"Because how would I explain why we are there?" Sara asked.

"Okay, so why don't we just go around the block and I'll check it out."

"Okay."

Chloe patted the back of the front seat. "Alright, Raul. Take us around to the hotel front entrance."

The cab took off again.

"How do you know his name?" Sara whispered to Chloe.

"It's on the card on the visor."

"I'm really good at this investigative stuff, aren't I?" Sara chuckled.

A few minutes later, they pulled up to the front of the historic and expensive Cameron Hotel. The large entryway to the hotel was clogged with other cabs so their cab pulled in almost a block down from the entrance. Chloe went to check it out. It was almost ten minutes before she returned.

"If she's in there I didn't see her. She's either left or is up in a room."

Sara looked out the window toward the hotel and sighed. "That's where she must be with whomever she's seeing."

"So, you think they're up there?" Chloe also looked out the window.

"It doesn't make sense that she would go in one entrance and out the other."

"Unless she thinks someone is following her and she's trying to throw them off."

Sara looked at Chloe. "Seriously, hello. We're the only ones following her, and she doesn't know that."

"At least you hope she doesn't know we're following her."

"I need a drink." Sara slumped in the seat.

"Okay." Chloe tapped on the glass. "Raul, we give up. Take us to Clancy's on West 76th."

"You got it," he said.

They sat in silence as the cab pulled away.

Chapter Thirteen

SARA ARRIVED SLEEPY-EYED at the brownstone the next morning. Having been disappointed in their spying skills, she and Chloe shared a bottle of wine at Clancy's as they attempted to piece the evening together. The conclusion remained the same. Claire had spent the evening at the hotel with the mystery man. Sara surveyed her desk and found nothing of urgency, so she called Claire on the intercom.

"Morning, Claire. I'm here." No response. "Claire are you sleeping?" Nothing. "Okay, I'm coming up."

Sara hung up the phone and made her way up the stairs. She stopped on the second floor and called out to Mrs. Hanson. No answer. *That's odd. Mrs. Hanson isn't here.* She continued upstairs to Claire's bedroom. The door was open, and Sara peered in. She was surprised to find the bed was already made up. *That's strange. She didn't have any early appointments.* "Claire?"

Sara walked to Claire's bathroom. As she looked around, she noticed Claire's makeup still out on the counter. She picked up a bottle of perfume. She waved the bottle a few times in front of her nose to inhale its scent before setting it back on the counter.

"She never came home," Sara said out loud as she stared at herself in the mirror. She walked back into the bedroom. *That's why the bed is made. She never slept in it last night.* Sara touched the bedspread. She stood there a moment, not quite sure what to do. When Claire was dating Michael, Sara knew when they would be spending time together and she never had to worry. But this secret relationship was freaking her out.

She took one more look around before going back to her office. Sitting at her desk, she stared at the phone. *Do I call her? I can't call her. What would I say? Where are you? Maybe I should call Abby. Oh, that would go over well, she hates me as it is. I can't call her to find out where Claire is. Not a good idea.* She did the next best thing—she called Chloe.

"Hello?" A groggy voice answered.

"Chloe, it's me. Are you still asleep?"

"Not anymore. What's up?"

"Claire never came home last night."

"Really?"

"Yes. I came in and no one is here. I went upstairs to find that the bed hasn't been slept in and her make-up from last night is still on the bathroom counter."

"Lucky girl." Chloe chuckled.

"Eww, Chloe."

"What? She obviously spent the night with someone. I told you."

"I know, but..."

"But what?" Sara heard Chloe yawn. "Look, she'll tell you what's going on when she's ready. In the meantime, be patient. Call me and let me know when she gets back."

"Okay. I'll talk to you later." Sara hung up the phone and got to work. She tried to concentrate while she watched the clock.

Nine, ten, and then eleven o'clock, nothing. Finally, at eleven-thirty Sara heard a car outside. She jumped out of her chair and went to the window. She moved the curtain back to get a better look. It was the black town car. The same driver got out, came around, and opened the back-passenger door. Still wearing the red cape and black beaded dress from the previous evening, Claire got out of the car. After saying something to the driver, she headed for the door.

Sara practically fell over her desk as she tried to get back in her chair. She heard the lock turn and the door open. Claire came in and hesitated inside the foyer. *Should I call out to her? No. Just sit here like normal and see what she does.* Sara picked up the first piece of paper she saw and looked at it as though it was something important.

"Good morning, Sara," Claire said from the doorway.

"Good morning, Claire." Sara looked up from the paper.

"I hope you weren't worried. I really should have called," Claire said as she pulled off her cape. Her hair and make-up were not as fine-tuned as the night before, but she was still stunning.

"You don't have to call me, Claire. I mean, I was worried, but I'm sure that I shouldn't have been. You have Abby and she knows where you are all the time so why should I?" *Oh, God, shut up. Stop talking.*

Claire came into the office. The black beaded dress was more gorgeous than Sara remembered. Moving some papers over, Claire sat on the corner of the desk. "Well, I apologize anyway. I should have let you know."

"I guess I was surprised that Mrs. Hanson wasn't here since she's always the first one in."

Claire got up. "Oh, yes. She had an appointment this morning. I guess I forgot to tell you that as well. I don't know where my mind is lately. I'll go upstairs to shower and change. I'll see you in a bit."

"Alright."

A few minutes later Sara noticed that Claire's cape was still on the chair. *Might as well bring this up and get a glass of water while I'm at it.* As she climbed the stairs, she decided to drop the cape off first and get the water on the way down. She would check the fridge and see what there might be for lunch. When she reached the doorway to Claire's bedroom, she heard her speaking to someone.

"I know, darling. It was a wonderful evening. I hated to leave. I can't wait to see you again. I don't want to take a shower since I can still smell your perfume."

Sara stopped in her tracks. *Perfume? Did she just say perfume?*

Claire laughed. "I can smell it all over me. I love that you were able to pick it up while you were in London. I know it's so hard to get here in the States."

Sara stood frozen, afraid to move and not wanting to call attention to herself. Suddenly, she felt a sneeze coming on. As hard as she tried, she couldn't contain it. She sneezed. She backed away from the door hoping that Claire would think she just got there. She heard Claire move toward the door.

"Can I call you back later? Yes, I will. Sara?"

"Yes. I have your cape."

"Thanks, darling. I...I was just finishing up a call," Claire said as she opened the door wider and took the cape from Sara's hand.

"Oh, really? I thought you might be in the shower already."

"Just about to get in. I'll be down in a little while."

"No problem." Sara turned and went down the stairs, completely bypassing the second floor, and forgetting about water and food. *Perfume? She must have misspoken. She must have meant cologne.* Her thoughts were interrupted by the front door opening.

"Hello," Abby said as she placed some paperwork on the desk.

"Hi."

"Can you separate these and bring them up for Claire to sign?"

"Sure."

"Are you alright?" Abby cocked her head at Sara, her brow crinkled.

Sara sat up straighter in the chair. "Yes, I'm fine."

"Okay. Is she up there?"

"Yes. She got back a few minutes ago and was going to get in the shower."

"Great. Bring the papers up when you have them organized." Abby left the office and Sara heard her heels clicking on the stairs as she went up.

Sara tried to shake off what she heard Claire say and concentrate on the paperwork. She had some other things to go over with Claire as well. When she got everything together, she made her way up the stairs. She found Claire and Abby sitting in the living room. Claire was dressed in a pair of jeans and light camel color sweater. She had some light make-up on and her blonde hair was drying from the shower. Sara sat down on the sofa facing Claire and Abby.

"So, things went well, I take it?" Abby asked Claire.

"Very well." Claire sighed. "But more on that later. What do you have for us, Sara?"

Sara handed the paperwork to Abby for her to go through each item with Claire.

"Anything else?" Claire asked.

"That does it for me." Abby took the papers and put them in her briefcase.

"And, my darling, what do you have for me?" Claire looked over at Sara.

Sara went through what she had which included some mail and phone messages. "Do you need anything else?" Sara asked Claire when she was done.

"No, thanks, darling. Abby and I are just going to catch up a little. I don't have any plans this weekend that Abby can't help me with, so you don't have to worry about that. Have you eaten lunch yet? You should go look in the fridge and get something."

"No, I haven't. I'll see what's in there and go back to the office."

"Please, darling. I worry about you not eating."

Sara laughed. "Thank you, Claire, but I do eat. You may not see me, but I do."

"Alright. I don't think you've been feeling well lately and you're not telling me, so I want to make sure."

"I'm fine, really." Sara picked up the papers and headed for the kitchen. As she left, she heard Abby whisper something to Claire, and Claire whisper back, but she couldn't make out what was said. In the kitchen, she grabbed a bottle of water and one of Mrs. Hanson's premade salads from the refrigerator.

"There now, that's better." Claire smiled at her as she came back into the living room.

Sara smiled back. "I'll be downstairs if you need me."

Back at her desk, she opened the salad and started to eat as she looked out the window. Her thoughts drifted back to the perfume comment and she decided she would discuss that further with Chloe.

A couple of hours later Abby came down and left. Sara looked at the clock and was surprised to see it was four o'clock. Sara hadn't made any plans for the evening, so she decided to call Chloe to see what her plans were. As she picked up the phone, she heard music coming from upstairs. *I guess Claire is relaxing.* Chloe didn't answer so she left a message.

Sitting back in her chair, going through some fan mail, Sara realized the music hadn't changed. *Why is Claire doing this? Is she alright up there?* Sara went and stood at the bottom of the stairs. *She must have played it five times already. What is going on and what is that song?* Sara concentrated on the melody and some of the words hoping it would come to her. Just when she thought she had it, the music stopped, and she heard Claire's footsteps cross the floor. Sara went back to her desk. A little after five o'clock she called Claire to tell her she was leaving.

Gail Newman

Chapter Fourteen

THE WEEKEND WAS UNEVENTFUL as Chloe had a date for both Friday and Saturday night. Sara busied herself cleaning and catching up on laundry. Sunday, they met at their favorite brunch spot, Finley's. They elected to sit at the bar near the window so they could people-watch as they ate. Sara brought a newspaper and Chloe brought a magazine so they could scour the latest news and gossip once they were done catching up with each other.

"So, how were your dates?" Sara asked once they got settled.

"The one on Friday was okay. I didn't really connect with her. But the one last night was good. This is the second time I've been out with her. You really need to let me set you up with someone, Sara. There are a lot of nice girls out there."

"If there are, how come you haven't found one yet?"

"I'm having too much fun looking." Chloe laughed. "You're more of a homebody. I think it would be nice for you to meet someone."

"I have things I want to do first."

"Yes, I know. Is it finish writing or start writing that screenplay?"

"Ha, ha. I have ideas...I just need to do it."

They ordered drinks and decided on eggs benedict. When they finished eating, they ordered another round of drinks while Chloe opened the newspaper.

"Oh my God, I almost forgot. What happened with Claire?"

After driving herself crazy most of the weekend, Sara had promised herself she wasn't going to bring it up unless Chloe did. Deep down she knew she wouldn't be able to keep that promise so she was glad Chloe brought it up first.

"She came home Friday morning looking almost as good as when she left. She gave me a line about how she should have called and then she went upstairs."

"That was it?"

"No. She left her cape on the chair in my office, so I took it upstairs. When I got to her bedroom door, I heard her on the phone telling someone what a great night it was, how she hated to leave, and how she didn't want to take a shower because she could still smell the perfume on her."

"Perfume? What perfume? Don't you mean cologne?"

"I know. That's what I thought, but she definitely said perfume." Sara nodded.

"Then what?"

"I sneezed, and she caught me on the stairs. I said I was just coming up and thought she was in the shower already."

"So, you let it go?"

"Yes. Abby came over and we did some work. After she left, Claire started playing this song over and over. I didn't realize it at first, but she played it about five times before she stopped. I left right after that."

"What was the song?"

"I'm not sure. I've been wracking my brain all weekend."

Chloe grabbed a pen that was sitting on the bar.

"Go ahead. I'm pretty good with this stuff."

Sara did her best to hum the tune and sing some of the words she remembered.

"Okay, so we have, 'I'll be waiting in the usual place' and 'There's no escape,'" Chloe said as she looked at the napkin she was writing on. After a few minutes of not coming up with anything, Chloe did what all good detectives do and looked it up on the internet.

"Holy shit." Chloe held up her phone to Sara.

"I can't see it. What does it say?"

"It's a Bryan Ferry song called 'Slave to Love.'"

"I don't get it." Sara took a long sip of her drink.

"What do you mean you don't get it? It's about a woman and meeting her in the usual place."

Sara took another drink. "I still don't get it." Sara shrugged her shoulders.

"Claire is seeing a woman."

"Get out of here. That's impossible."

"Really?" Chloe folded her arms. "Mystery date, perfume, and now this song?"

"Give me your phone." Sara held out her hand.

She read the lyrics. Then Chloe read the lyrics. Then they wrote the lyrics on the front and back of another napkin. After another round of drinks and several more rounds of reading the lyrics, they came to the only conclusion they could. Claire was seeing a woman.

"Wow." Chloe sat back in the barstool. "This is big. If this gets out, this is going to be big."

"Gets out? Gets out? How is anything going to get out?" Sara started to panic.

"If we figured this out, someone else will."

"We only figured this out because I had inside information and you and I aren't telling anyone, right?"

Chloe didn't say anything.

"Right, Chloe? You're not going to say a word about this. Promise me, Chloe."

"Alright, alright. I won't say anything."

"Pinky swear." Sara held up her pinky.

"Seriously? Do I have to do that?"

"The only way I can trust you is with a pinky swear because you know I will break your pinky if you break my trust."

"Fine." Chloe held up her pinky.

"Pinky swear we don't say a word about this to anyone," Sara said as they curled their pinkies together.

"So, what happens now?" Chloe asked as she signaled for another round.

"Nothing, I guess, until I find out more." Sara sighed.

They turned their attention back to the newspaper and their drinks. Sara checked one side of the page while Chloe checked the other.

"Oh. My. God," Chloe said.

"What?"

Sara stretched her neck to see the page Chloe was looking at. "Well, looky here." Chloe pointed at the page.

"What? Tell me."

"'Well known French actress Claudine Monet has taken up residence for the time being at the Cameron Hotel. Ms. Monet is in town after finishing a film shot in London.'"

"Okay. So, what does that mean?"

"Don't you know who Claudine Monet is?"

"No."

"She's a French actress and she's a lesbian, a very beautiful French lesbian."

"So?" Sara started to get the picture. "Wait, you think Claire was meeting this chick?"

"Well, if she's seeing a woman, and she was in that hotel at the same time, it makes sense."

"Get out of here. Is there a picture?" Sara grabbed the paper.

"No, but I'll find one." Chloe picked up her trusty phone and, after a moment of clicking keys, handed it to Sara.

"Wow." Sara's eyes got wide.

"See? I told you. Beautiful, right?"

"I'll say," Sara said. *I wonder why Claire hasn't told me. Guess I know where I stand.* Sara's heart sunk. "Good for her. If that's who she's into now, then good for her," Sara said, deciding she didn't want to share the disappointment she felt with Chloe.

"I hope you get to meet her." Chloe was still looking at her phone.

Sara slapped Chloe's hand.

"What? You got to meet Michael. Why wouldn't you get to meet her?"

"Because I don't know anything about this and, at this rate, she probably won't tell me. Let's just relax and finish the rest of our day."

"Can you imagine if Claire Elliot is seeing Claudine Monet what a media frenzy that would cause? The press will go crazy for this." Chloe shook her head.

"Really, Chloe, this is all just speculation on our part. I mean, short of them going out in public on an actual date, we probably won't have any proof. I may have misheard the whole perfume remark."

"Look at you backtracking." Chloe laughed.

"I'm just saying we don't have any hard evidence."

"What about the red bra?"

Sara wanted to forget about that.

"Seems to me that would be something a French woman might wear." Chloe smiled.

"Maybe. I don't know."

"Just keep your eyes and ears open when you get to work Monday morning. Have you heard from Claire at all this weekend?"

"No." It was a little strange that there wasn't an email, text, or call from Claire about something. Not wanting to seem too upset, Sara tried not to make too much of it.

"I think Abby had everything covered for the weekend."

"Covered up sounds more like it." Chloe bumped Sara's shoulder with hers.

"Great." Sara shook her head.

"Why don't we change the subject and see what else is going on in the world," Chloe said, turning the page.

They resumed their reading and finished their afternoon. On the way out, Sara put the napkin with the lyrics on it in her pocket.

Chapter Fifteen

SARA ARRIVED AT WORK to what seemed a usual Monday morning. After she checked her desk for anything urgent, she went upstairs. Mrs. Hanson was in the kitchen prepping and cooking items for the week. She had a pot of tea and a plate of pancakes ready for Sara. She sat and chatted with Mrs. Hanson while she ate and then grabbed another mug of tea to take downstairs with her.

As she turned to go back downstairs, she saw them. A large vase with beautiful multi-colored flowers sat on the cocktail table. She went to get a better look at them and scanned the blossoms for a card. She found it nestled close to one of the flowers. Carefully she pulled it from its place and looked at the envelope. "Claire" was all it said. Inside, the card had a few simple words. *Tell her I'll be waiting in the usual place.* It was signed Claude. Sara heard Claire coming down the stairs. Fumbling, she got the card in the envelope and back into place just as Claire entered the room.

"Good morning, darling. Aren't they beautiful?" Claire stood behind her.

"Yes, they are. I couldn't help but want to smell them."

"I know. I've been doing that since they arrived." Claire leaned down to smell the flowers. "Nothing like a beautiful vase of flowers to brighten a room. Did you have a nice weekend?"

"Ah, yes. Nothing special. Cleaning, laundry, and brunch with Chloe."

"How is Chloe doing?" Claire asked, turning to look at Sara.

"I'd say she was doing well. She had two dates this weekend."

"My, my. Let me get my tea and let's sit down. I want to hear all about it."

Sara stood staring at the flowers until Claire returned.

"So." Claire settled on the sofa. "How does one date two women at the same time?"

That's a curious question. Sara turned to face Claire.

"I think Chloe has eliminated one since she said she didn't feel any chemistry with her. The other was a second date, so she might want to see how that plays out."

"Where does she meet these women?"

"Through friends or at work. Being a make-up artist, she meets a lot of people. In fact, she wants me to start dating again."

"Really?" Claire put her teacup down. "How do you feel about that?"

"I don't know. At first I wasn't interested but I've been thinking about it and it might not be such a bad thing to get out there a little more."

Claire ran her fingers through her hair. "It can be hard to meet people. The bar scene certainly isn't the way to go. But if friends introduce you, or you work together, at least you might start with some common interests."

"Is that how you meet people, Claire?" *There. Let's see how she handles this.*

Claire picked up her teacup up and stood up. "I...I've met people both ways, I guess."

"Your relationship with Michael...I guess that was through work?"

Claire started to circle the room. "Yes."

Sara was about to ask another question when she heard a phone ringing. Claire reached into the pocket of her sweater and pulled out her cell phone. "I'm sorry, darling. I have to take this call." She quickly left the room and went upstairs.

Sara sat down on the sofa. *Damn, I almost had her...maybe.* She stared at the flowers for a few more minutes. She was about to get up when Claire came back in.

"Sara, darling, I've got an event Thursday evening. Would you be a love and call the dry cleaners and see if my black pinstripe suit will be ready?"

"Of course. I'll call now and let you know."

"Also, Abby won't be able to attend with me, so I'll need you to come."

"I can do that."

"Thanks. You're a love."

Claire went into the kitchen and Sara went down to the office. She called the dry cleaners and made arrangements for the suit to be delivered.

Sara returned to the living room where Claire was sitting and joined her on the sofa. "Your suit will be ready. Are you sure you don't want me to call around and get you something new?"

Designers clamored for Claire to wear one of their designs to big events. If she thought the event called for it, Claire would ask Sara to call one of her favorite designers for a loaner for the evening. But the clothes that Claire bought were always stunning and sometimes she liked to wear something already in her closet.

"No, darling, that's fine. This is a small awards event for independent screenwriters. This year it's being held here in New York. One of my friends was nominated and asked that I attend. I don't think there will be much press or anything like that, but it should be a nice gathering."

"Will there be an area where I can wait for you?"

"Actually, darling, I thought you might like to sit with me."

"I'm sorry, sit with you?" Sara wasn't sure she heard Claire correctly.

"Yes, sit with me. You have an interest in screenwriting and I thought you might enjoy it. Maybe get your interests stirring again."

"I'm surprised you remember."

"Oh, come now. It may not always seem like I'm paying attention or that I remember things but believe me, I do."

"I don't know what to say." Sara blushed.

"Just say that you will come."

"I already did."

"Ah, but that was when it was about work. This will be as my guest."

"Thank you, Claire. That would be very nice." Sara took a slight breath to calm herself.

Claire grabbed Sara's hand. "Wonderful, darling. Now don't worry about a thing. You know what I'm wearing. You can wear whatever you are comfortable wearing. The car will pick you up at six o'clock."

"Is there anything else I should know? I mean I've never been to anything like this except behind the scenes."

"There will be a small step and repeat. You know where you stop for the photographers to take pictures. You can walk with me if you like."

"Oh no. I don't think so." Sara shook her head.

"Alright then, you can go through and I'll join you inside. Is that okay?"

It sounds quite wonderful. She couldn't hide her smile. "Yes, that sounds great."

Claire was still holding Sara's hand and gave it a slight squeeze before letting go.

They went back to business as usual, but Sara could only think about two things—*I can't wait to call Chloe and what the hell am I going to wear?*

Chapter Sixteen

"I REALLY DON'T THINK this should be so hard," Chloe said as she stood outside the dressing room where Sara was changing.

The moment Sara got home Monday evening she was on the phone to Chloe about the event. They planned to meet on Tuesday right after work at a boutique where Chloe was sure Sara would find something she liked.

"Look, I know you think I'm crazy, but this outfit has to be just right." Sara was putting on another dress that Chloe had pulled from a rack. "No, I hate it." Sara put it back on the hanger. "Could you please get me that outfit I showed you?"

"Fine, I give up. You can try it on."

As soon as they walked into the store Sara spied an outfit she loved. She wanted to try it on right away, but Chloe directed her elsewhere.

"Okay, here you go." Chloe handed it to her through the curtain.

Sara slipped into the outfit and stood in silence staring at herself in the mirror.

"Well, what do you think? Are you coming out or should I just slowly slide down the wall and sit here?"

"I think we might have a winner."

"Really? Come out and let me have a look."

Sara stepped out of the fitting room wearing a black ruffled three-quarter length skirt and a black and white off the shoulder blouse. She carried the pashmina which completed the outfit.

"Wow, Sara, look at you. I have to say I never would have picked this for you, but I think it looks great." Chloe circled Sara.

"I know it's weird, but when I saw it, I thought if nothing else I'd try it on for shits and giggles. But I like it. What do I do for shoes and accessories?"

"I'm seeing some simple black pumps and no jewelry except maybe some simple earrings. If you'd like, I'd love to do your hair and make-up."

Sara stared at herself in the full-length mirror. "Okay, but not too much."

"Seriously, no one knows you better than I do. I think I can handle it."

Sara took one more look before heading back into the dressing room to change. "Great, let's get it and go."

* * *

Sara got home and hung the outfit on the back of her closet door. She kept going back in the bedroom to look at it, questioning if she made the right decision. She knew she had when she felt herself smiling about it as she fell asleep.

Wednesday morning, she was sitting in her office reading the mail when Claire appeared in the doorway and startled her. "Oh my God, Claire, you scared the daylights out of me. I didn't hear you coming." Sara put her hand on her chest.

"What exactly does that mean, darling? I have never understood that saying."

"I'm not really sure but it beats some of the others I could use."

"Sorry. I thought perhaps you heard me coming."

"I didn't, so give me a moment for my heart to stop pounding."

Claire came in and sat in the chair across from Sara. "Are you ready yet?" A little smile crept up her face.

"Fine. I'm sure my heart will eventually stop beating so hard, but if you must, go ahead."

"No. I'll sit here and wait." Claire began to wiggle in her seat. "Are you ready yet?"

"Really, Claire, what's with you?" Sara was starting to smile.

In a small voice Claire said, "I just wanted to make sure you are still going with me tomorrow night."

Sara laughed out loud. "What is that? A voice you're trying for a movie?"

Claire kept wiggling in the chair and again in the little voice said, "No, although perhaps I can use it somewhere. Are you still coming with me tomorrow night?"

"Yes, Claire, I am still coming with you tomorrow night."

"Goody," Claire said in the little voice as she jumped up out of the chair.

Sara sat back in her chair laughing as she listened to Claire run up the stairs.

Chapter Seventeen

THE EVENT BEGAN AT seven o'clock and the car was picking Sara up at six o'clock, so she left the office at four in order to get home and get ready. Chloe was waiting on the sidewalk in front of her apartment when she arrived.

"Okay, you get in the shower and I'll set up my stuff," Chloe said when they got inside. She immediately began unpacking her make-up and hair equipment.

Sara stopped to look as she headed to the bathroom. "Are you going to use all that stuff on me?"

"Well, I don't know. If you're going to start complaining already, I'll use it all plus anything I can find in the kitchen. Go get in the shower."

Sara emerged a few minutes later to find Chloe ready for her. She had moved one of the kitchen chairs into the small living room.

"Have a seat." Chloe motioned toward the chair. "I'll start with your hair first."

"Now, don't do anything that's going to make me not look like me," Sara said as she sat down and looked up at Chloe.

"I think I got this, Sara. All I am going to do is highlight your natural beauty."

"Don't cut my hair." Sara grabbed Chloe's hand.

"I'm not going to, you big baby. I can do more than just make-up."

Chloe went to work. Sara had no mirrors to look in, so she had to wait until Chloe was done. After a few minutes of brushing and blowing, Chloe stepped in front of Sara

"I think that will do."

"Let me see."

"No way. You have to wait until I put the make-up on."

"But suppose I don't like my hair?"

"Does it feel any different? Are you in any pain?"

"No."

"Then shut up and let me work." Chloe started with Sara's eyes. "Okay, look up. Now look down. Close your eyes. Look up and to the left."

"Chloe, I don't think my eyes will do that."

"Yes, they will, just follow my finger."

"Is this what women do every day?" Sara fidgeted in her chair.

"Yes. Sit still. I don't want to poke your eye out."

"Could that happen?" Sara started to get up, but Chloe put her hands on her shoulders.

"Sit still. I think you are my worst client ever." Chloe pushed Sara back into the chair. "Let me put a light brush of foundation on, a bit of light lipstick, and we'll be done."

"I don't look fake or clownlike, do I?"

"Yes, Sara, I'm going to let you go out looking absolutely ridiculous." Chloe put the lipstick down, looked Sara over, and then picked up a mirror. "Ready?"

"Yes." Sara grabbed the mirror. Slowly she raised it to her face. She was met with a beautiful reflection of herself. "Wow."

"I do good work, right?"

"Chloe, I don't know what to say." Sara felt tears well up.

"No, no. Don't cry. You'll ruin everything. Here." Chloe handed her a Q-tip with a tissue wrapped around it. "Make-up artist secret...if you feel like you are going to cry just dab this in the corner."

"I'm okay." Sara dabbed the Q-tip in each corner of her eyes. "Seriously, this looks like me, just better." Sara held up the mirror. "I've got to go look in the bathroom mirror." Sara jumped out of the chair and headed for the bathroom with Chloe on her heels. "Chloe, I don't know what to say."

"Dab, please. Something along the lines of I'm a brilliant artist will do."

"You are. I mean, I've seen your work, but look what you've done to me."

"Sara, all I did was add some color, blend, and fluff you up a little more. The rest is all you. You're beautiful. You just have a hard time believing it."

"Thank you, Chloe. I love you." Sara turned and hugged her.

"That's what besties are for." Chloe returned the hug. "Now, let's get you dressed."

"What time is it?" Sara took one more look in the mirror before heading for the bedroom.

Chloe was already taking the outfit off its hanger. "It's a quarter to six."

"Are you kidding me?" Sara started to panic.

"Look, it's better to be ready right on time than to sit and wait."

"Good advice." Sara nodded.

"I know. Here's some more...go pee." Chloe waved her hand back in the direction of the bathroom.

"What?"

"Go pee now because as soon as you put this on, you'll have to go and then we'll have to get the skirt off and back on you."

"But I can just lift the skirt up."

"You can do that later. For now, go before you get dressed."

"With what you have done for me today, I won't question anything else you tell me to do. But that's just for today." Sara grinned as she closed the bathroom door.

"That's fine. I can deal with that."

Sara emerged from the bathroom and they finished getting Sara dressed.

"Here are your earrings and shoes." Chloe handed the earrings to Sara and placed the shoes in front of her.

Sara put the earrings on before slipping the shoes on her feet. She stood up and looked at Chloe. "So, how do I look?"

"You look amazing." Chloe's eyes welled up with tears.

"Really?"

"Really. Amazing. Come look."

Sara moved in front of her full-length mirror and had to agree with Chloe—she did look amazing. "I can't believe that's me."

Chloe stood behind her and wiped the tears from her eyes. "Believe it, because it's true." She walked to the window and looked down to the street. "It's time."

"Is the car here?" Sara asked, still looking at her reflection.

"Yes."

"Oh boy. Now if my legs would just move, I'll be good to go."

"Come on," Chloe said as she put her arm around Sara's waist and directed her toward the front door. "Here's your purse. You have everything you need in it. Your phone, a small brush, and a small sample of the lipstick in case you need to reapply."

"Will I need to do that?"

"You do what you feel comfortable with. Now take a deep breath and just try to think that you are going to a movie or something with a friend."

"Yes, but this is an event and I'm going with a movie star."

"Calm down. You're going to an event with a friend."

"Okay. I'll keep repeating that all the way there."

Chloe led her out the door and down the stairs to where the car was waiting. As soon as they appeared on the steps, the driver jumped out to open the door.

"Good evening, Ms. Burton. My name is John and I'll be taking care of you this evening."

"Hi, John. Nice to meet you. This is my friend, Chloe."

"Good evening, miss. Are you all set, Ms. Burton?"

"Yes, I think so." She looked at Chloe for confirmation.

"You are good to go." Chloe gave her a hug and whispered in her ear. "It's just an event with a friend."

Sara returned her hug. "An event with a friend," she repeated as she let go of Chloe and got into the car. As the car pulled away, she turned to wave at Chloe.

"We should get you there right on time, Ms. Burton." John glanced over the seat toward Sara. "I've been told that you might not want to arrive at the front entrance where the press is. Would you prefer I drop you off where some of the other guests are arriving that's not as high profile?"

"That sounds like a great idea. I'm not somebody that anybody cares about, so no need to make a big entrance."

"Hey, now, we are all someone to somebody." John smiled at Sara as he looked at her through the rearview mirror.

"I guess you could be right about that, but for now, I'd prefer the lesser entrance." Sara looked out the window.

"Okay."

The rest of the ride was silent as they made their way to the theater.

"Are we almost there?" Sara asked as the car slowed down.

"Yes. I'll pull over to let you out in just another minute. You have to walk up the street a bit and go through the theater's side entrance. It's close to the main entrance so you can get inside and watch people arrive."

Sara's heart started to beat faster.

After John parked, he turned and looked at Sara. "I'll be here to pick you up unless Ms. Elliot's driver calls to let me know you're going with them."

"Oh, I didn't think that far ahead."

"You don't have to. We have you covered. Ted will let me know what you decide."

"Thank you, John." Sara smiled.

"No problem. Let me come around and help you out." He jumped out of the car and came around and opened the door. He reached in to take Sara's hand. She looked at his hand waiting for hers. She flashed back to when she watched Claire as she took the hand of the driver that helped her from the car when she and Chloe followed her to the hotel. Trying to be just as elegant as Claire, she took John's hand and allowed him to help her out of the car.

"I hope you have a wonderful evening, Ms. Burton."

"Thank you, John."

Stepping away from the car, she turned to get her bearings. She could see people crowding the sidewalk and walked in their direction. As she approached the front of the theater, she spied the side door entrance and noticed some of the press turn in her direction as she made her way to it.

"Good evening. May I have your name please?" a woman with a clipboard asked.

"Sara Burton."

The woman scanned the sheet.

"Yes, Ms. Burton, here you are. You're a guest of Ms. Elliot."

"Yes, I am." Sara smiled.

"Wonderful. Would you like to have someone take you to your seat or would you like to wait here for Ms. Elliot? Or you can stand over there and see her as she comes in."

"I'll go through and wait. Thank you."

"Have a nice evening," the woman called after her.

Sara moved to where the woman had gestured for her to wait for Claire. Looking around, she took in the grandness of the theatre. The theatre was built in the 1920s and renovated over the years to keep its original beauty.

A few people made their way through the main entrance with the press snapping their pictures as they arrived. Claire was right. It was tame compared to some of the events Sara had been to with press yelling to get the attention of the stars and fans vying for autographs and pictures. *I can handle this. It's just an event with a friend.*

She caught sight of a black town car pulling up to the entrance. The driver came around, opened the door, and placed his hand inside. A moment later, there she was. Claire smiled as she got out of the car. Stunning as usual, she wore the black pinstripe suit with her blonde hair slightly curled like a 1940's movie star. The small crowd went wild. Cameras and cell phones pointed at her as she made her way up the red carpet, smiling and waving. She once told Sara that she wouldn't stop for autographs for fans at events that weren't for her. That was for the people for whom the event was being held. People were speaking to her as she came in the door and as she answered them, she looked around. Finally, her eyes met Sara's. Her smile grew wider as she made her way toward her.

"Look at you, my darling." Claire shook her head as she grabbed Sara's hand. "I thought it was you, then I wasn't sure. But it is you, and I'm just speechless. Well, I guess I'm not speechless as I can't stop talking. You look so beautiful. Just beautiful, darling. I'm just...I'm just, blown away is all I can say."

Sara blushed. "Thank you, Claire. It's all a little out of my comfort zone but it's just for the night."

"I hope it's a long night then, as I...I just can't stop looking at you."

"You look stunning, as usual."

They were saved from having to say anything else by a waiter passing around champagne. "Would you ladies like a glass?"

"Yes, thank you." Claire took two off the tray and handed one to Sara. "Cheers," she said as they clicked glasses. "Were you alright getting here?"

"Yes. The driver was very nice."

"Claire, how good of you to come." A tall, handsome man joined them and kissed Claire on the cheek.

"It's so good to see you, Peter. I'm so excited for you," Claire said as she placed her hand on his shoulder. "Peter, I'd like you to meet Sara Burton. Sara, this is Peter Harper. He's one of the nominees this evening."

"It's very nice to meet you, Sara." Peter gently took Sara's hand and kissed it.

"Thank you. It's nice to meet you, too."

"Peter, Sara is an up and coming screenwriter." Claire smiled at her.

Sara felt her cheeks blush. "No, not really. It's just a dream of mine."

"You know, my dear, dreams can come true. If you do decide to do something, please let me know. I'd love to give you any guidance that I can." Peter smiled.

Claire grabbed Sara's hand. "We might take you up on that, Peter."

"Anything for you, Claire. Now, if you ladies will excuse me, I have others to speak with before this starts. Thank you for coming, Claire, and very nice to meet you, Sara," he said as he turned and vanished into the crowd.

"Really, Claire? An up and coming screenwriter?" Sara frowned.

"I'm sorry, darling. Did I upset you?"

"I'm not a screenwriter," Sara whispered.

"If you want to, you could be. Why don't you start thinking and acting like one?"

"Is that what you think? That if you think and act like something you can become it?"

"Oh, bloody hell I do. How do you think I became an actress? I had to think and act like one. The rest you learn. But, my darling, if you don't get it into your head what you want, it will never happen."

Sara stared at Claire for a moment. In the year she had known Claire, this was the most insight she had given Sara about her career.

"I don't know what to say."

Claire seemed a little taken back by her declaration as well. "You can be anything you want, Sara. Just don't settle. Do you remember how we first met?"

"Yes," Sara answered, slightly confused.

"You were taking classes in midtown. Studying screenwriting, if I remember correctly, and I had just had my first movie released."

"I saw a flyer that you were going to be interviewed on campus and I went with some friends."

"I was very nervous." Claire smiled and shook her head.

"Nervous? You could have fooled me. First, you seemed to float effortlessly across the stage while wearing a pair of stunning stilettos. Then you were so at ease with the questions that were asked. You listened intently and thoughtfully to each person, even bantering back and forth with them."

"It might not have seemed like I was nervous, but I was at the start. Then I decided they were just nice people asking questions because they were interested."

"Even now, I hear how the press loves to interview you because you are engaging and have a quick wit."

"I do, don't I?" Claire flicked her hair back with a wave of her hand.

"I think that's why I felt comfortable enough to come up and ask you a question."

"Yes, I remember. You had on that lovely black jacket I admired."

Claire ran her hand down Sara's arm as if she were touching the jacket. "You asked a very good question about when I was looking at scripts, if I preferred a newly written screenplay or something that had been adapted from a play or book."

"I can't believe you remember that, Claire." *All I remember is I was locked on those beautiful blue eyes that were looking at me.*

"Do you remember what I said?"

"Sort of."

"I said that if I was lucky enough to go forward with the career I had chosen, that hopefully, I'd have a chance to find out the answer to that question. Then I asked if you were a screenwriter."

"You did, and I said I hoped to be and was taking some classes." Sara smiled at the thought.

"I asked if you would stay behind so we could talk a little longer."

"Yes, and when you came back out to meet me, the first thing you asked was 'so what are you writing?'"

"And what did you say?"

"That I just had some thoughts and stories that I hoped would one day turn into something more."

"That's when I had my brilliant idea." Claire threw her hands up in the air.

"That I should be your assistant." Sara laughed. "How could I be your assistant when you didn't even know me or my name?"

"You told me your name and I gave you my private number and I wouldn't take no for an answer."

"I remember looking at the card when I got home. Your number was on one side and Abby's was on the other side. When I called the next morning, while the phone was ringing, I was rehearsing my speech about why I couldn't possibly take the job but what a nice offer it was."

"And?" Claire smiled broadly.

"And I couldn't get a word in edgewise and that's how I came to be your assistant."

"See, darling, that's why you have to take chances. You never know how things will turn out." She linked her arm through Sara's. "Now, let's see what else is going on here, shall we?"

"Alright." Sara smiled.

"Come on now, you can do better than that. I tell you what, let's have another glass of champagne and I'll introduce you to some other people as Sara Burton, a work in progress."

"Oh no you don't." Sara grabbed Claire's hand and laughed.

They stood there smiling at each other and Sara let go of Claire's hand. "Another glass of champagne would be nice. Perhaps you can tell me about Peter's work, and maybe some of the others as well, so I know a little more for the evening."

"Fair enough," Claire said, signaling for the waiter.

Claire gave Sara an overview of the film for which Peter was nominated and what she knew about some of the others. People stopped to greet her while they spoke. She exchanged hellos with them but never took her attention away from Sara for too long. The lights flickered to let them know that the show would be starting soon and an usher escorted them to their seats.

Sara was intrigued with each piece and its writer and found herself silently rooting for the ones she found interesting. Claire would occasionally lean over and whisper some information about the nominees or movies.

Peter Harper won the award he was nominated for and Sara and Claire enthusiastically applauded for him. When the awards ceremony was over, they made their way back to the lobby. Again, people stopped Claire along the way to ask about current or upcoming projects. Finally, they made it to a quiet corner.

"Sara, would you like to get a drink with me?" Claire looked away and then back at her. "We could go somewhere, just the two of us. Or if you prefer, I'm sure there's an after party somewhere."

Sara suddenly felt very shy, but before she could answer, Peter interrupted them.

"Ladies, I hope you will join us over at the Cove for a little party."

Claire looked at Sara as she said, "Thank you, Peter. Sara and I were just discussing our plans."

"Claire, why don't you go? I have some things to take care of and I don't want to keep you from going."

"Sara, I—"

Sara didn't let her finish. "Please, Claire, you go on. Congratulations, Peter."

Sara walked away as Claire called out to her, "Sara, please don't go."

Sara kept moving, working her way through the crowd in the lobby and finally to the street. Not sure of what to do, she headed in the direction of where the car had dropped her off. She was halfway down the street when someone spoke to her.

"Ms. Burton?" John was leaning against the town car. "Can I help you?"

Sara stopped in her tracks. "Yes, please, John. Can you take me home?"

"Of course, Miss."

He opened the back-passenger door and Sara slid in. Her heart was pounding. She hadn't realized tears were flowing down her cheeks until John handed her a box of tissues after he got in the car.

"Are you alright?"

"Yes, I'm sorry. I'm fine. Just a little overwhelmed from the evening."

"Let's get you home."

They drove in silence and before Sara knew it, they pulled up in front of her building. John opened the door and helped her out. "Is there anything else I can do for you?"

Sara was touched by his compassion. "No, thank you, John. I'm okay. Really. Thank you again for taking care of me this evening."

"It was my pleasure." He waited outside the car until she was safely inside the building.

She breathed a sigh of relief as she opened the door to her apartment. She took her phone from her purse and looked at it before she set it on the table. She had a missed call from Claire. She sat down and started to cry again. *What is wrong with me? I was having a nice evening with Claire and could have continued it. Why did I run?* She sat back in the chair and cried herself to sleep.

Chapter Eighteen

SARA WAS AWAKENED THE next morning by the sound of her alarm clock going off in the bedroom. As she opened her eyes, she realized she was still in the chair and dressed from last evening. She got up and made her way into the bedroom. After she turned off the alarm clock, she hung her skirt, blouse, and pashmina back on their hangers. Entering the bathroom, she caught sight of herself in the mirror. Mascara streaked across her face like war paint. She got in the shower and let the warm water wash it away.

Following her usual morning routine in somewhat of a daze, she got dressed and left for work. As she walked along her usual route, she thought back to the last moments of the previous evening. It had been a wonderful evening, and when she saw Claire, she would thank her. Hopefully that would be the end of it until she had a chance to figure out what upset her so. She jumped when her cell phone rang. Not looking to see who it was, she answered.

"Hello?"

"Hey there. I thought you would have called me by now. So how was it?" Chloe asked.

"It was good."

"That's it?"

"It was good until I freaked out and left." Sara stopped at a corner and checked for oncoming traffic before continuing.

"What?" Chloe gasped.

"I freaked out and left. I don't know why."

"You have to know why. What happened?"

"I was having a very nice time, but then, after the ceremony was over, Claire asked if I wanted to go get a drink with her, just the two of us. Or we could go to the after party."

"What was wrong with that?"

"I don't know but I felt weird about it. Claire had introduced me to one of the nominees as a screenwriter and that freaked me out. After that it felt weird to hang out with those people."

"You could have gone and had a drink with Claire, and you wouldn't have had to hang out with them."

"I know. I felt weird about it and I ran out."

"Why didn't you call me? I would have come over."

"I know. I got home and cried myself to sleep."

"Sara, we are really going to have to work on your self-esteem. I mean, this was Claire. What did we say before you left? 'This is just an event with a friend.'"

"That is until your friend arrives and is treated like a movie star."

"Was it like that?"

"No, not really. She was very cool and low key and she really did pay attention to me."

"Where are you now?"

"On my way to work."

"Do you have a plan?"

"Yes. Thank her for the evening and then not discuss it anymore."

"Gee, let me know how that goes." Chloe laughed.

"What do you mean?"

"Don't you think she's going to ask you why you ran away? I'm surprised she didn't call you."

"She did. I missed a call from her."

"I think, there's a pretty good chance you are going to have to talk about this."

"Look, I'm almost there. I'll call you later."

"Good luck," Chloe said as she hung up.

Sara looked up at the brownstone before climbing the stairs and letting herself in. In her office, she hung up her jacket and put her pocketbook away. She sat down at her desk and looked around. *Oh, why can't it be yesterday morning again? I would have done things differently. What would I have done differently? I would have gone for a drink with Claire. I have to fix this. I need to tell Claire that I was feeling a little out of place and that I should have accepted her invitation.* She heard footsteps coming down the stairs and steeled herself. *Okay here's my chance.* But it was Abby who appeared in the doorway.

"Good morning, Sara."

"Hi. I didn't expect to see you here this morning."

"I had some things to take care of while Claire's gone. Would you make two copies of these, please?" Abby handed Sara several sheets of paper.

"Of course. What do you mean, while Claire's gone?" Sara asked as she took the papers.

"She decided to go away for the weekend. She'll be back some time Monday. Bring those up when you are done, then I have some other things I need help with."

"Sure."

Abby turned and went upstairs.

Sara sat and looked at the papers. Claire hadn't said anything about going anywhere. *She would have told me.* Sara wracked her brains to think if she had heard anything about Claire going away. *No, I would remember, and Claire would have reminded me last night. Where did she go and why?* She went to the copier and ran the two sets of copies. *There's only one way to find out what's going on,* she decided as she made her way to the living room.

Abby sat on the sofa, paperwork scattered on the table in front of her.

"Here you go," Sara said as she handed the papers to Abby. "Can I do anything else for you?"

"Possibly. I'll have to let you know. I hadn't expected Claire to go away, so I have some things to sort through."

"I didn't think there was a planned trip. I didn't know anything about it and Claire didn't say anything last night. Is everything alright?"

"Yes. Everything's fine. She got a last-minute invitation and decided to take advantage of it," Abby answered in an annoyed tone

"Alright, then, as long as everything's okay. I'll be in the office if you need me."

"Thanks."

Sara called Chloe when she got back to her office.

"So, what's up?" Chloe asked as she answered her phone.

"Abby is here and seems slightly pissed. Apparently, Claire got a last-minute invitation to go away for the weekend."

"You mean she's not there?"

"Nope. She must have left really early."

"Wow."

"I know, right?"

"Any idea of where she went?"

"No, but I'll see if Abby says anything today, although I don't know how long she'll be here." Sara moved some paperwork on the desk.

"Maybe she's gone off with Claudine."

"Why would you say that?"

"Why not? Maybe she did."

"I'll call you later."

"Okay, bye."

Sara put the phone down and looked around. *There must be a clue upstairs somewhere. I just have to find it.* She tiptoed upstairs and peeked around the corner to see where Abby was. She was sitting in a chair by the window, talking on her cell phone. Sara listened for a minute, but she could tell it wasn't Claire she was speaking to. When she heard Abby say she would be leaving in a few minutes, Sara crept back down the stairs to the office.

A few minutes later Abby appeared in the doorway. "I'm off. If you need anything just call my cell."

"Thanks. Have a good weekend."

As soon as Abby was out the door Sara flew up the stairs. After checking the living area, she moved to Claire's bedroom. *Surely if there is anything at all, I'll find it there.* Standing in the doorway, she felt like she was trespassing. *It's not the first time I've had to look for something in this room. It's just that Claire didn't ask me to this time. Oh well, a girl's gotta do what a girl's gotta do.*

She checked the bathroom first. The counters were clear of make-up and everything else. Back in the bedroom, she checked the tops of the dressers. They were clear except for picture frames and various decorative items. She looked around the room, her eyes coming to rest on the nightstands. The first one she checked contained a few books, but the other one revealed some paperwork in the drawer. For a split second she hesitated but then looked at the first sheet. It was a "things to do" list. The second sheet of paper looked like the beginning of a note. She took it out of the drawer and began to read.

"I suppose I might have misjudged your feelings toward me. Maybe I'm not the person you thought I was. I'm willing to try if you give me another chance."

That's it? Sara looked at both sides of the paper. That was all it said. Studying it, she thought she saw the faint imprint of a letter at the top. It looked as though Claire started to write but hadn't clicked opened the pen. *What letter is it?* She ran her finger across the front and back of the letter. When she couldn't figure it out with her fingers, she turned the lamp on and held the note up to it. *Is that a C? It looks like a C. Chloe was right. Claire has gone away with Claudine, hoping for another chance.* Sara sat down on the edge of the bed still holding the note. *Well, that explains her sudden absence.* She took one more look at the note before placing it back in the nightstand. She went back to the office and finished out the day before heading home.

Chapter Nineteen

SARA RETURNED TO WORK on Monday and found no sign of Claire. A note from Abby said that Claire would be returning at some point during the week. *Claire is obviously enjoying her time away with Claudine.*

Wednesday afternoon the phone was ringing as Sara entered the office after running errands. She grabbed the phone from the other side of the desk as she put down the mail. "Hello?"

"Good Afternoon. This is Elaine calling from the Cameron Hotel. I'm calling to confirm that Ms. Elliot wants to keep her dinner reservation for tomorrow evening."

"I'm sorry?"

"Ms. Elliot has a dinner reservation for tomorrow evening in her room. We want to confirm that is still her plan."

"I'm sorry, is Ms. Elliot staying at the hotel?"

"We usually check on these types of requests twenty-four hours prior to the reservation."

"May I have your number, Elaine? I'll have to call you back to confirm." *So, Claire is somewhere but is checking into the hotel again on Thursday evening. I guess I'll call Abby and see what she has to say.*

Abby answered her cell phone on the second ring.

"Yes, Sara?"

"I'm sorry to bother you, but Elaine from the Cameron Hotel just called to confirm dinner reservations for Claire tomorrow evening. She said that Claire hadn't checked in yet, but since she requested dinner in her room, she was calling ahead to confirm."

"Did you get the number?"

"Is Claire back?" Sara asked after giving Abby the number.

"I'll handle this, Sara. Thanks for calling."

Abby hung up and Sara stared at the phone in disbelief. *What the fuck is going on?* Sara sat down at her desk and looked around. *This is just crazy and I'm on the crazy train and need to get off at the next stop. Enough. I have got to talk to Claire and find out what's going on. Talk to Claire? How can I talk to Claire when I don't know where she is or when she's coming back? One thing's for sure. My alcohol consumption is growing with all this going on.*

***

"You know, I like Finley's well enough, but we could have had drinks at the Plum Room at the Cameron. Then we could have taken our drinks and sat in the lobby to see who comes in." Chloe's swizzle stick clinked on the sides of her glass.

"What will that prove? It's not like Claire is going to come walking in." Sara sipped her martini.

"Maybe she would. She might check-in tonight instead of tomorrow."

"Look, all I can do is ask Claire what's going on. I mean, this is just crazy. She has appointments scheduled. I don't know what Abby is doing about those. There are things to do with the movie she just finished, and she vanishes."

"Oh, come on now. You're not concerned about that. You want to know what's going on and with who." Chloe put her drink down and looked at Sara.

"Yes, that's true. But I also never got to explain to her what happened the night of the awards ceremony."

"I don't think she's worried about that anymore."

"What do you mean?"

"I mean, if she was worried she would have contacted you. You said you had a missed call from her that night. She didn't leave a message, then she left, and you haven't spoken to her since. I think she has more going on than worrying about you." Chloe lifted her drink and tipped it towards Sara.

Sara stared at Chloe. "Gee, thanks for that low blow."

"What? I didn't mean it like that. We're trying to figure out what's going on and it looks to me like she is having a relationship with Claudine. Everything is hush hush. They probably have to lay low while they decide how they are going to handle the publicity."

"That's what you think is going on?"

"I do, and I think that Abby's nerves are frayed with this whole thing." Chloe took a sip of her drink.

Sara pondered what Chloe said for a moment. "I guess you could be right."

"I think I am. It all kind of makes sense." Chloe nodded.

"I think you may have something there. I guess my role is to continue to be the faithful assistant. If Claire wants to tell me what's going on, then she will. I'll do whatever she needs me to do, as usual."

"There you go." Chloe patted Sara on her back. They toasted to it and spent the rest of the evening discussing other things.

Gail Newman

Chapter Twenty

SARA SPENT THURSDAY CONCENTRATING on the things at hand. She vowed to stop thinking about what Claire was up to. *Nope. I'm not going to think about if she's checked into the Cameron yet. Who she was with or where she has been.* To distract herself, she decided to do a little window shopping on the way home. It was a beautiful evening as she strolled along one of her favorite streets, lined with small boutiques and bookstores. She jumped when her cell phone began to ring. She fumbled to get it from her jacket pocket and answered without looking at it.

"Hello?"

"Hello, my darling. How are you?"

"Claire?" Sara couldn't believe her ears.

"Yes, darling, it's me."

"Claire, I wasn't—"

"I know you weren't expecting me. Did I catch you at a bad time?"

"No. I'm just walking down Harrison Street. Where are you?" *Why did I ask that*? Sara mentally smacked herself.

"That's why I'm calling, darling. Do you think you could do me a favor?"

"Of course, Claire. What is it?"

"Do you think you could come to the Cameron Hotel?"

Sara started looking for a cab. "Yes, I can do that. Claire, are you all right?"

"I'm fine. I'm in suite 1209. You'll need to come up the private elevators. They are down the hall on the right from the lobby. I'll let them know that you are coming. Just give the elevator operator your name."

"Alright. I'm on my way."

"Thank you, darling."

After they hung up, Sara hailed a cab. She checked her phone and saw it was almost eight o'clock. A few minutes later the cab pulled up in front of the hotel. After she paid the cabbie, she stood for a moment looking up at the hotel. She made her way through the revolving doors into the lobby. It was a grand old hotel and, at any other time, she would have loved to stop and take it all in, but right now she was on a mission. As she headed down the hallway to the private elevators, one of the doors opened. An older, stately gentleman emerged, and Sara moved to take his place within.

"May I help you?" the elevator operator asked

"Yes. My name is Sara Burton. I'm expected."

"Of course, Miss. You are going to suite 1209."

"Yes, thank you."

They rode up in silence until the elevator stopped. "1209 is right down this hallway on the left, Miss," the operator said as he stepped outside.

"Thank you." Sara smiled at him as she exited the elevator.

"Have a good evening," he said as the elevator door closed.

Sara turned and went down the hallway, looking at the numbers on the doors as she passed each one until she stood in front of 1209. As soon as she knocked on the door it opened and there stood Claire, beautiful as ever.

"My darling, here you are."

She opened her arms to embrace her. Sara walked into them and returned the hug.

"It's so good to see you," Claire said as they broke apart.

"You as well, Claire. I was worried about you."

"Me? Oh, there's nothing to worry about. Come in and sit down. Would you like a drink? I've got a lovely bottle of wine to open."

"That sounds nice."

Claire turned her attention to the wine while Sara looked at her surroundings. The suite was gorgeous. It had floor to ceiling windows that she was sure overlooked a fabulous view. Two lovely gold colored sofas faced each other in the middle of the room surrounded by glass top tables, all of which had fresh flower arrangements on them. On the left sat a glass dining table with color-coordinated fabric on the chairs to match the sofas. All the fabrics and colors, from the furnishings to the paint on the wall, blended to make a stunning room. There was also a fireplace along one wall. The bedrooms appeared to be down a hallway to the left of the dining area.

"Sit down, darling." Claire handed Sara a glass of wine as they sat together on one of the sofas.

"So," Claire patted Sara's knee, "How are you?"

"I'm fine. Everything's good." *This is so weird. I haven't seen or heard from you in over a week and here you are acting like I just came over for a glass of wine.*

"Wonderful. I'm sure everything is fine at the office?"

"Yes, everything is fine there."

"Good, good." Claire sipped her wine. "Have you eaten, darling?"

Sara took a sip of wine. *Okay, let's see where this is going.* "No. I was window shopping and hadn't thought of eating."

"Perfect. I have dinner coming up in a few minutes. You simply must join me."

"I'd love to. Thank you."

They sipped their wine in silence as Sara waited for Claire to say something.

"Tell me, darling, how is Chloe?"

"She's fine, being her usual self." Sara smiled.

"Is she still balancing dates?"

"No. I think she is just seeing one girl. In fact, they are on a date this evening."

"Really? How wonderful. Are they out for dinner?"

"Dinner and a movie I believe."

"What movie?"

"Gee, Claire, I don't know. There are some good movies out there right now and I don't know which one they picked." *Why are we making small talk about Chloe? Why am I here? What the hell has been going on?* Sara wanted to ask but knew she wouldn't.

"Yes. Yes, there are." Claire sipped her wine.

"Speaking of which, do you have anything I need to take care of for the film you just finished?"

"Abby has that all in order."

"Okay. I'm sure she'll let me know if she needs my help." Sara lightly tapped the side of her glass with her fingernail.

"Of course she will. You know she thinks very highly of you."

Sara chuckled. "She hasn't tried to kill me while you've been away. I guess that's a promising sign."

Claire laughed as well. "Maybe I wasn't gone long enough."

"Thanks, Claire," Sara said, tilting her head to one side.

"Only joking, darling."

"Speaking of being away." *Might as well ask.* "When do you think you'll be back?"

"I'll be there when you get in on Monday morning. I have been remiss, and I have a busy week ahead. Abby has had to shuffle my schedule."

"I thought as much. Claire, I want to thank you for the evening at the awards show and I want to tell you—" Sara was interrupted by the ringing of the doorbell.

"Dinner is here." Claire jumped up to answer the door.

Sara watched Claire glide elegantly towards the door. She greeted the two waiters as they brought the cart of food in and made their way to the dining table. After a quick exchange, Claire sent them on their way.

"Would you like another glass of wine before we eat, or shall we go to the table?"

"I'm fine with whatever you would like to do, Claire."

"I am a little hungry so how about I fetch the bottle of wine and we eat?"

"That's fine." Sara rose from the sofa and went to the table.

A place setting was at each end of the table. She was unsure where to sit until Claire directed her.

"Sit here, my darling." Claire motioned toward a chair.

Once Sara was seated, Claire poured more wine in her glass before taking her seat and refilling her own glass. She raised it toward Sara.

"Thank you for coming, my darling. I have missed you."

"I've missed you too."

They each took a sip of their wine before uncovering the dish in front of them. A fabulous aroma arose from the plate.

"Goodness, Claire, this smells wonderful. What is it?"

"Beef Bourguignon. I can't resist having it when I'm here."

This could be my opening. But before she could start, Claire continued.

"I love the gravy and the potatoes and the asparagus. I have had it elsewhere, but I think the chef here makes it the best. Anytime I'm in the restaurant, I have to have it. You know it's one of Julia Child's most famous recipes."

"I think I heard that." Sara picked up her fork.

"Do you like to cook, Sara? I do. I just never get the time."

"In the year I've worked for you, I don't think I've ever seen you cook." Sara laughed.

"Well, darling, you haven't seen me on the weekends. The weekends we have been together we have been in a trailer or a hotel."

"That's true. I'm not that good of a cook. On the weekend I usually go out or Mrs. Hanson sends food home with me."

"Mrs. Hanson is a very good cook. Perhaps I'll have to cook for you one evening."

"Really, Claire? You would cook for me?" Sara smiled.

"I'm serious, Sara."

"I'm sorry. I guess I just never thought of that happening."

Claire put down her fork and looked at Sara. "I am a woman of my word."

"I didn't say you weren't. I guess I don't see us hanging out together. I mean, I work for you."

"I thought we had more of a relationship than that." Claire seemed surprised.

"Well, maybe I'm not just your typical assistant. I mean, I think I'd take a bullet for you." Sara didn't want to hurt Claire's feelings.

Claire started to laugh. "What do you mean, you think?'"

"You know, if for some reason you were being shot at, I might try and push you out of the way. It depends on how close I was to you at the time and what I was doing." Sara was laughing too.

"So, you mean, if you weren't doing something else important, and a bullet was heading my way, you might make the effort to get me out of the way or get in front of me?"

"Yes. Getting in front of you would all depend on where the bullet might hit me. Arm or leg, yes, but any vital organs and you might be on your own."

They were laughing so hard they had tears running down their faces. Claire picked up her napkin and wiped her eyes.

"Alright, so I see where this is going. We need to be better friends. So, I'll ask you some questions."

"You probably don't know a lot about me." Sara wiped her eyes.

"Of course, I do. You were born in Boston and have two brothers."

"I was born on Long Island and have two sisters."

"Ah ha, see, I was kidding. Your sisters are Emma and Madalyn."

"Actually, they are Emily and Madison."

"Are you quite sure?" Claire sat back in her chair.

Sara picked up her wine glass and took a long drink. "Yes, pretty sure that's who I grew up with. At least you got their first initials correct."

"Oh." Claire frowned.

"It's really okay, Claire. I don't expect you to know a lot of personal things about me. It's not how our relationship is."

"I do know that that your favorite color is blue, your favorite flowers are sunflowers, and that you secretly and will never admit it, love 80's music."

"Not bad. Yes, I would admit that I love 80's music, but I would admit that only to certain people." Sara nodded.

Claire waved her finger at Sara. "See, I do know you. I remember other important things, like about your love life."

Sara flashed back to the conversation they had in the car weeks ago. "And we are not going to discuss that any further."

"Nothing new on that front?"

"Nothing to report."

Claire sat looking at Sara.

Here's my chance. Sara put an elbow on the table, rested her chin on her palm, and leaned toward Claire. "What about you, Claire? Anything new on that front?"

"What do you mean?"

"I mean, are you seeing anyone?"

Claire's facial expression told Sara she was getting uncomfortable with the direction the conversation was going. "No. Nothing going on. I've been too busy."

Sara could see the relief on Claire's face when her cell phone began to ring. "Excuse me for a minute, darling."

She pulled the cell phone from her bag and looked at it. She hesitated, her finger poised above the screen, but then placed it back in the bag and returned to the table.

"Are you still hungry? I'm sure there's more." Claire gestured toward Sara's plate.

"No, thank you. That was delicious. Is everything alright, Claire?"

"Yes, of course. Why don't we take our wine into the living room?"

Sara got up from the table and started to stack the plates off to the side of the table.

"That's alright, darling. Leave it there. It will be picked up later."

"Sorry, old habits die hard." Sara turned and made her way to the window. It proved to be as spectacular a view of the city as she expected. She was standing there looking out, lost in the view, when she felt Claire come stand behind her.

"Magical, isn't it?"

"I've always loved to look at the lights of a city. I kind of think you can get a real feel for it when you see it lit up at night."

"You should see Paris. Have I ever taken you there?"

"No."

"Someday."

Sara could feel Claire's soft breath as it sighed past her. Her spine began to tingle.

"Did you do a lot of traveling growing up?" Claire walked to the sofa and sat down.

Sara turned away from the window. "Up and down the east coast, but not overseas or anything like that."

"Why was that?" Claire motioned for Sara to join her on the sofa.

"I think it was easier for my parents to throw the three of us girls in the car and drive," Sara sat down.

"Did you enjoy those trips?"

"Oh yes. We always had the best times. My mother was, well still is, a housewife or homemaker or whatever the proper term is these days. As soon as my father knew when he was going to take vacation, they would plan somewhere for us to go and we would all climb into the car and off we would go. What about you, Claire? Growing up in Australia sounds so exciting to me."

Claire reached for the wine bottle and refilled both of their glasses. "It was fun, probably like your childhood."

"I would have loved to have brothers. I mean, you have three, but at least you have a sister, so you had choices." Sara tucked her feet under her on the sofa.

Claire's glass was midway to her lips, but she stopped and smiled at Sara over the rim. "I bet you can name my siblings, can't you?"

"Sure. You have Richard, Robert, Andrew, and your sister Jane."

"I'm impressed although, I guess, not surprised."

"Come on, Claire. It's not like I haven't shopped for them or spoken to them on the phone. I feel like I know them even though I haven't met them in person."

"No, they haven't been to the States."

"But your Dad was born here, wasn't he?"

"Yes, in California. His family left when he was a small boy. His father took them to Australia for a job position and they never left."

"Then he grew up and met your Mom and they had all of you."

"Yes, and my Mum was not about to leave her homeland." Claire waved her finger in the air.

Sara felt as though she was being swallowed up by the sofa and struggled to move.

"Can I help you out of there, darling?"

Claire put her glass down and grabbed Sara by the elbow to pull her up. Their cheeks brushed against each other as she did, and Sara felt that tingling again.

"I should probably get going, Claire. I don't even know what time it is." Sara looked around the room for a clock.

"Are you sure, darling?"

"Yes, I'm sure. It's getting late and I have to get a cab and..." Sara lost her train of thought.

"I have a better idea."

Claire reached toward Sara. Thinking Claire was going to embrace her, Sara panicked and slid off the sofa onto the floor.

"Sara, darling, are you alright?" Claire kneeled next to Sara.

"I guess the wine went to my head."

"Let's get you back on the sofa." Claire took Sara's elbow and helped her up. "You need to sit here for a moment. Or maybe you need to lie down."

That's the last thing I'm going to do after you just made a move on me. "No. Really, I'm fine. I should just be going."

"Are you sure?"

"Yes. I'm fine."

"Let me call a car for you." Claire reached behind Sara and picked up the hotel phone. "Hello, this is suite 1209. Would you please have a car brought around for Ms. Burton?"

Wow. What kind of idiot am I? She wasn't making a move on me. She was reaching for the phone.

"The car will be out front in a moment." Claire took Sara's hand. "Are you sure you're alright to get home?"

"I'll be fine, Claire." Sara rose from the sofa and walked to the door. "Thank you. This was nice."

"Thank you for coming. Please call me when you get home." Claire followed her.

"I'll text you so that I won't disturb you."

"You won't be disturbing me. I'll be worried until I hear from you, so you will call me the moment you get in the door." Claire pointed her finger at Sara.

"Okay, I will." Sara opened the door and turned to look at Claire. "Claire, I wanted to tell you that I had a good time with you at the awards ceremony. I would have loved to have gone with you for a drink, but I was a little overwhelmed."

Claire rested her head against the door. "You would have?"

"Yes. Yes, I would."

"But you rushed off so quickly without any explanation. I thought I'd done something wrong."

"No, Claire, you didn't. I guess, I was just a little overwhelmed by the evening."

"I'm sorry you didn't tell me." Claire gently touched Sara's cheek.

"I'm sorry that I didn't."

Sara smiled and then turned and went to the elevator. As she went through the main lobby door, a bellman asked if she needed transportation. She told him there was a car waiting. After asking her name, he led her to a black limousine.

Arriving home, she called Claire.

"Home safe and sound?" Claire asked when she answered her phone.

"Yes, I am."

"Good night, my darling."

"Good night, Claire."

Gail Newman

Chapter Twenty-one

CLAIRE WAS AT THE townhouse Monday morning as promised. The rest of the week, she and Sara had tea each morning, and in the afternoons and evenings Abby whisked Claire off for appearances and meetings.

Thursday afternoon, Sara felt she could come up for air. When she looked at the clock, she was surprised to see it was almost six o'clock. She locked up the brownstone and walked out into the cool evening. Autumn had fallen upon the city. Kids had gone back to school weeks ago, leaves were turning color, and chrysanthemums and pumpkins were appearing on doorsteps. Sara breathed in the cool air and stopped to button her jacket. Since Chloe was working, she decided to walk and enjoy the evening. She stopped at a corner bistro. *What a lovely night to sit outside and have a drink.*

She ordered a glass of Pinot Noir, sat back, and watched people stroll by. Her waiter returned with her wine and lit the candle that sat in the middle of her table. She sipped her wine and listened to the soft music playing in the background. She was lost in thought when she realized her cell phone was ringing. Checking the caller ID, she saw it was Claire.

"Hello, Claire," she answered in a sing-song voice.

"Hello, Sara. Sounds like I caught you at a good time."

"Why, yes, you did. I'm at a beautiful café, enjoying a nice glass of red wine." Sara picked up the glass and admired its contents.

"Are you on a date?"

"A date? No, I'm alone." Sara took a sip and set the glass onto the table.

"You sound so relaxed, and since you are at a café having wine, I thought you might be having a nice time with someone."

"I am relaxing, but it's because it's a beautiful evening out, not because I'm with someone."

"Then I certainly don't want to bother you."

"Claire, you're not bothering me. Are you calling just to say hello, or did you need me to do something?" Sara picked up the glass and swirled the wine.

"Well, calling just to say hello would be nice, wouldn't it? But I did want to see if you could do something for me."

"What would that be, Claire?" Sara laughed.

Claire hesitated for a moment. "Could you come to the Cameron Hotel?"

Sara took the phone away from her ear, looked at it, and then put it back. "Come to the Cameron?"

"Yes. Suite 1209. You remember what to do from last time."

"I do."

"Thank you, darling. I'll see you when you get here."

Sara shook her head as she disconnected the call. She took her time and finished her wine, paid the bill, and hailed a cab. Before she knew it, she was knocking on the door of suite 1209. A moment later, Claire opened the door and ushered Sara in with a wave of her hand.

"Thank you so much for coming, Sara. I wasn't sure what to do."

Sara closed the door behind her and then noticed the tissues Claire clutched in her hand. "Claire are you alright?"

"I'm fine, darling. Just being silly I guess."

"What are you being silly about?"

Sara pulled off her jacket and set it and her bag on a chair. Looking around the room, she saw that there were flowers on the table and the dining room table was set for two, just as it was the previous Thursday evening.

Claire had her back to Sara. As she turned around, she wiped her eyes and dabbed her nose with the tissues. Her mascara was smeared and her nose was red. It was obvious she had been crying.

"It's nothing. Would you be a darling and undo this zipper for me? I need to change into something else."

Claire turned her back to Sara and lifted her hair out of the way. Sara began to unzip the dress. The sight of Claire's white skin caused her to slow down. *It looks like it would be so soft to touch.* When she realized Claire wasn't wearing a bra, she began to blush. *Why is this bothering me? I've helped her change a thousand times.* She pulled the zipper down the rest of the way and then tapped Claire on the shoulder.

"All done," she said softly.

"There's a bottle of wine in the chiller. Would you mind opening it? I'll be back in a moment." Claire moved toward one of the bedrooms.

"Sure."

Sara took the wine from the ice and began removing the foil. She glanced around the room as she did. *So, Claire is here for what now, the third or fourth Thursday in a row? I've been here today and last week. Who's supposed to be here that's not showing up? Claudine Monet, that's who.*

She went to her bag and pulled out her phone. Sara thought that Chloe was probably home by now and would be all over it as soon as she saw the text message Sara sent: *See if you can find out where Claudine Monet is right now.* Chloe's answer was fast. As far as she could tell, Claudine was still in New York. Sara dropped her phone back into her bag and went back to the wine bottle. She got the cork out just as Claire reappeared. She had changed into a pair of jeans and a soft, colored blue V-neck sweater. She sank into the sofa.

Sara poured the wine and joined her. As she was handing a glass to Claire, she was trying to think of something to say but Claire beat her to it.

"Do you think you might like to stay for dinner with me?"

Sounds more like a plea than a request. "I guess I could."

"Thank you." Claire took a deep breath and sipped her wine.

Sara took a sip of her wine as well and they sat quietly for a few minutes. "Claire are you alright?" Sara asked when she couldn't stand the silence anymore.

"What do you mean?"

Sara placed her wine on the cocktail table and turned to Claire. "What I mean is, you seem to be preoccupied with something or someone."

Claire put her hand up. "Someone? Why would you say someone?"

"I'm not specifically saying someone. I'm asking you if you're alright and maybe, if something is wrong, I can help you."

Claire put her glass down and turned to Sara. "Would you help me?"

Sara took Claire's hand. "Of course, Claire. There isn't anything I wouldn't do for you."

Claire began to cry.

Sara pulled her into an embrace. "Claire," she whispered into her ear. "I don't know what's going on, but I'm always here for you."

Claire pulled back and looked at Sara. She reached up and caressed Sara's cheek. As if in slow motion, Sara felt Claire coming closer to her, and then she felt Claire's soft lips on hers. Sara felt like she was dreaming. Her head was spinning as the kiss became deeper. All she could feel was the softness of Claire and the smell of her perfume.

Claire pulled away and jumped up. "Oh my God, Sara. I'm so sorry!"

It took Sara a moment to regain her composure. Claire seemed more surprised than she was. "Claire, it's fine. I mean it's okay." *Shut up. Don't start blabbering.* She stood up and went to Claire.

Claire stood with her back to Sara.

"Claire, look at me."

After a moment, Claire turned to face her. "I'm so sorry, my darling. I don't know what got into me."

"It's alright, Claire. Why don't we sit back down? Let's have some wine and calm down."

"I'm so embarrassed. I don't know what to say."

"Just sit down. It's fine. Really, it is."

Sara went back to the sofa and sat down. When Claire joined her, Sara handed her the glass of wine, picked up her own glass, looked at Claire, and drained the glass. Claire followed suit as Sara picked up the bottle to pour them refills.

"Now, why don't we just continue on with the evening?" Sara smiled at her. *If I don't freak out, hopefully Claire won't either.*

The doorbell rang and Sara went to answer it. The waiter had arrived with their dinner. Sara instructed him to place the food on the table and sent him on his way.

"Do you want to sit for a moment, or shall we eat?"

"Perhaps some food would be in order." Claire stood and went toward the table.

Sara retrieved the glasses of wine from the cocktail table and placed them at their table settings and then removed the covers from their plates.

"This smells fabulous. What is it?"

"It's Lobster Newburg." Claire picked up a fork full. "You're not allergic to seafood, are you?"

Sara laughed. "No. No, I'm not."

"Oh, thank God. I would hate to think that I almost killed you twice this evening." Claire laughed.

"I'm fine, Claire. I'm a lot stronger than most people think."

"You are always surprising me." Claire looked thoughtfully at Sara.

"Why do you say that? I don't do anything surprising."

"I think you do. You always find the good in people and you can handle any situation."

"I don't know about that part." Sara shook her head.

"Yes, you do. You take care of me, you run the office, and when something goes wrong, you fix it."

"I think Abby is the one that really takes care of you. Although I try. The rest is my job."

"But you see, that's the thing." Claire touched Sara's hand. "You have to be that way, you know, inside. Caring and loving in order to do the things you do. As for Abby, she does take care of the business side of me. And yes, she does care, but it's different. At least, that's how it's turned out to be." Claire turned her attention back to the food.

What does that mean? Abby's caring, but it's different than how it turned out? Sara was not sure if she should ask what Claire meant.

They chatted on and off until they finished eating and then retreated to the sofa.

"That was delicious. Thank you."

"You are most welcome." Claire refilled their glasses. "Sara, I really do appreciate you coming here on a moment's notice for me."

"There isn't anything I wouldn't do for you, Claire. But I am wondering why you're here on Thursday evenings and why you called me tonight and last week?" *Shit, why did I ask that*?

Claire looked at Sara and stood up. "I've been working on something and I'm still trying to see how it will all work out." Claire downed the rest of her wine and picked up the bottle to refill her glass. "It's required me to do some things that I don't usually do."

"Such as?"

"Needing to get away on fairly quick notice and being here. It's nothing for you to worry about. I'm fine."

"I don't know about that, Claire. You were awfully upset when I arrived."

"Nonsense. That was just me being foolish. Then there was that awkward moment with you, which my darling, again, I am so sorry about."

Sara patted the cushion on the sofa for Claire to sit down. Taking her hand once she did, Sara looked Claire in the eyes. "Claire, I was serious about what I said. There isn't anything I wouldn't do for you or to help you. If you find that, at some point, you want to share with me whatever is going on, please know I will keep it in confidence and never judge you."

"I appreciate that, Sara, more than you know." Claire patted Sara's hand before letting go.

They were both quiet for a moment. *Think of something to say to turn this conversation around.* "Dinner really was delicious. I don't think

I've ever had it before." *That was lame.*

"Yes, it was delicious," Claire said as she ran her hand under her chin.

Sensing this was a good time to end the evening, Sara stretched and let out a slight yawn. "It's getting late. I should be going."

"Of course, darling."

Sara picked up her bag and jacket from the chair and walked to the door as Claire followed. Sara opened the door and turned to look at Claire. "I meant everything I said."

"Thank you, my darling. I know you did." Claire smiled.

Sara walked out and closed the door slowly behind her.

Chapter Twenty-two

"WHAT DOES THAT MEAN, it was just a kiss?"

Chloe was lying on the floor of her apartment while Sara lay face down on the sofa. Having gone over the events of Thursday evening again and again, they hit the bar scene Friday night and were now paying for it on Saturday morning. Sara turned her face away from the pillow cushion just enough to get the words out.

"It wasn't anything. Claire was upset, and she just reacted."

"No. I'm sorry. Reacting for Claire should have meant crying on your shoulder, not kissing you. That doesn't make any sense. I'm telling you, she was upset about Claudine standing her up and it caused her to take her sexual frustration out on you."

"Chloe, I can't go over it anymore. My head hurts from thinking about it and from drinking about it."

"And she didn't say a word about it Friday?"

Sara struggled to sit up. "For the zillionth time, I saw her briefly before she went out and everything was as it always is. We talked about work, she wished me a good weekend, and she left with Abby for her appointments. I think I need food."

"Okay, I agree we need food. You go shower since you are more upright then I am. I'll lay here 'til you are done, then I'll shower, and we'll go in search of food."

Not wanting to risk the chance of getting car sick, they walked the short block to Murphy's Diner where they knew they could get a cure for what ailed them. Settling in a booth, they both ordered a hot tea, a glass of cola, scrambled eggs, and toast. Sara was relishing the silence until they were interrupted.

"Chloe? I knew it was you." Two women stood next to them.

Chloe looked up. "Hey there, Meg. How are you? It's been a long time."

"Too long. This is my friend, Lisa. Lisa, this is Chloe." Looking at Sara she said, "And I don't know you."

"Oh sorry, this is my friend, Sara."

"Hi." Meg turned her attention back to Chloe. "I haven't heard from you in a while. How come you haven't called me?"

"I'm seeing someone, so I haven't been out and about."

"Oh well," Meg said. "I guess we should run. Come on, Lisa. Good to see you, Chloe, and you too, Sara."

Meg turned to leave before Chloe or Sara could comment. Lisa turned towards them. "It was nice to meet you, Sara."

Sara looked up at Lisa. She was an attractive blond with bright blue eyes. "Yes, it was nice to meet you as well."

They shared a long look before Lisa turned and followed Meg out the door.

"That was interesting." Sara sipped her cola through a straw.

"I'll say." Chloe picked up a pack of sugar to add to her tea. "Meg couldn't wait to get out of here once I told her I was seeing someone."

"What was up with that? I mean you are sort of seeing someone, but that usually doesn't stop you."

"Yes, my friend, that might sometimes be true, but I would have told Meg I was married to get away from her. She is not my type at all."

"You didn't sleep with her, did you?"

"No. Thankfully. I never would have gotten rid of her then. But enough about me. I think Lisa had eyes for you."

"Really?" Sara raised an eyebrow.

"Ah, yeah. She took the time to stay behind and talk to you. I think that was a subtle move of interest."

"She was pretty."

"Could be a nice distraction."

Sara giggled. "I like the way you put things, Chloe, but I don't know anything about her except her first name."

Chloe signaled the waitress for another pot of tea.

"I could make some inquiries if you want me to. You know, just to see if she's involved with anyone and if she might be interested in meeting you some time."

"Oh, I don't know if I could do that." Sara shook her head.

"You're not doing anything. I'll find out if she's involved. If I find out she isn't, then you can decide if you want to meet up with her. No harm in that."

Sara thought for a moment. *I don't have anything else going on. It might be nice to go out with someone.*

"Okay, I don't see any harm in you finding out if she's involved with anyone. And by anyone, I mean not in a long-term relationship and if she's looking for fun dating. I don't want to have an upset girlfriend or boyfriend looking for me."

"I doubt that there is a boyfriend in the picture. Meg only surrounds herself with women who like women."

"Okay, you find out and we'll go from there. In the meantime, I need more tea and more sofa time."

By Sunday afternoon Chloe let Sara know that Lisa was single. They discussed the pros and cons of whether Sara wanted to meet her. Finally, after much deliberation, Sara agreed to let Chloe find out if Lisa wanted to meet for drinks somewhere.

***

Sunday afternoon Sara sat nervously playing with a sugar packet at a small coffee shop near Central Park. Two weeks had passed since Chloe was able to find out Lisa was single and interested in meeting Sara. Two Thursdays came and went without a phone call from Claire to come to the Cameron. Things remained quiet on that front. There were no last-minute disappearances, no whispering between Claire and Abby, just the usual rounds of post-production activities and new scripts being delivered.

It was during one of those quiet days that Sara got up enough nerve to call Lisa. Since Chloe had done some of the groundwork for her, Lisa was expecting Sara's call and accepted her invitation immediately.

Sara looked up each time the café door opened. She decided to concentrate on something else, so she turned her attention to the waiter who was pouring coffee beans into a machine. Hearing the sound of footsteps, she turned her attention back and found Lisa standing in front of her at the table.

"Hi, were you daydreaming?" Lisa asked as she sat down.

"Ah, no. I guess I just drifted somewhere for a minute."

"Isn't that sort of the same thing?" Lisa laughed, struggling to hang her bag on the back of the chair.

"I guess it could be argued on either account. Thanks for coming." *Why do I feel like crawling under the table?*

"Thank you for asking."

The waiter appeared to take their orders. Lisa settled on a cup of raspberry tea and smiled at Sara.

"I've never been here. It's quite nice."

"Yes, it has a comfortable feeling," Sara said, looking around.

"My friend, Chris, told me you're an assistant to a movie star. That sounds exciting. I'm not going to ask for whom. I understand confidentiality."

"I am, and I like it very much. It certainly has its moments though." Suddenly Sara flashed back to the kiss. She struggled to regain her focus. "I mean with schedules and things like that."

"So, do you do everything?" Lisa sipped her tea.

"Well, no. I mean, I do specific things like manage the office and mail. There's an agent and publicist and others that make the whole thing work. I do get to go on location and to events sometimes."

"That sounds interesting."

"It certainly can be." Sara thought back to the taxi chase. "Chloe tells me that you're studying to become a dentist."

"I am. Not a glamorous profession but it's something I've always been interested in."

"You certainly have nice teeth." *What a stupid thing to say.* Sara scolded herself.

"Thank you."

Say something intelligent. "Anything in particular that made you choose dentistry?"

"I've always wanted to do something in a medical type profession, one where I could work with kids. I looked into being a doctor, but that didn't quite seem the thing for me. When my sister started having kids, dentistry became an option."

"How so?" Sara poured herself more tea.

"I had to take my oldest nephew to a dentist appointment. My sister made me promise that I would go in the exam room with him for moral support. By the end of that appointment, I was hooked."

"How close are you before you can practice?"

"Right now, I'm on my third step, which is earning a dental degree. Then I have to get a license and go through residency. I already know that I'd like to be a pediatric dentist."

"That sounds like a lot of work. Maybe when you're done, you can get your sister's kids to be your first patients."

"Oh, no." Lisa laughed. "I don't want that responsibility. One false move and my sister would kill me. I'd be happy to help in an emergency, but routine appointments, no."

"How many siblings do you have?"

"Just the one sister, but she has five children so that's a handful in itself. What about you?"

"I have two sisters."

"Any nieces or nephews?" Lisa smiled.

"Not yet. Both are married but don't have any kids yet."

"Get ready, because when they do, they think because you're the unattached one that they can call on you for anything. Babysitting, chauffer for soccer games, the list goes on." Lisa waved her hand.

"Good to know. I'll be ready with my excuses." Sara laughed.

They chatted for the next hour and upon leaving, decided they would get together again.

***

"It was nice." It was Monday morning and Sara was in the office on the phone with Chloe.

"Details, girl, give me details."

"She was nice, and we decided to see each other again. I don't know, maybe dinner or a movie. I guess we'll just wait and see."

"Are you going to call her?"

"I called the first time. She can call me." Sara turned to pick up some mail when she saw Claire standing in the doorway. "Chloe, I'll call you later." Sara hung up without allowing Chloe to say anything. "Claire, I didn't hear you come down." She shuffled some of the envelopes.

"No problem, darling. I came down to see if that script had been delivered yet." Claire walked over and touched a paper on the desk.

"No. Nothing has been delivered yet. I'll bring it up when it comes."

"I couldn't help but overhear. Did you have a date over the weekend?"

"A date? Not really a date." Sara stumbled over the words. "I met someone for tea."

"One could consider that a date." Claire smiled.

"I don't know. I mean, we sort of met through Chloe. She seemed to like me, so we met for tea." Sara felt a small trickle of sweat bead up on her neck.

"Will you be seeing her again?"

Sara put the envelopes down and picked them up again. *Why is this making me so nervous? Just tell her yes, I am going to see her again.*

"I guess. Maybe. If she calls me, I'll go out with her."

"Sounds like you find her interesting."

"She was. She is. She's going to be a dentist." *Oh, dear God, shut up. Now you're just babbling.*

"My, my. A dentist. Sounds promising." Claire smiled and walked to the door.

"I...ah...I mean, I guess so."

"I hope it works out for you, darling." Claire turned and went up the stairs.

Sara sat down at her desk. *What just happened? Why did I get so nervous talking to Claire about this? The last time she brought up my love life I had the same reaction. Calm down. There's nothing going on, and even if there was, Claire will eventually have to know. Eventually,* Sara repeated as she got back to work.

Chapter Twenty-three

LISA CALLED WEDNESDAY AFTERNOON and invited Sara to dinner on Friday night. Thursday morning, Sara was sitting in the living room with Claire and Abby going over paperwork and Claire's upcoming schedule.

"Look, if you have no interest in the script, I'll tell them that." Abby stirred her coffee.

"I don't think it's the right project for me, but I hate to say no." Claire sighed.

"Not a big deal. It's not like there won't be another script arriving any minute." Abby looked at Claire, a serious look on her face.

"You're right. Let them know that I'm not interested and thank them for the opportunity," Claire pointed at Abby. "Be nice."

"What? I'm nice when I turn people down."

"Yes, Abby. I know how you can be, which is why I tell you to be nice."

Sara chuckled

"Excuse me. Do you have something to say about this?" Abby asked.

Sara looked up from her paperwork and was met with a fiery stare from Abby. "Me? No. I'm sorry I wasn't really paying attention." *Liar.*

"What were you thinking about then?" Abby asked.

Quick, come up with something. "Something this girl I met said on the phone about dinner tomorrow night." *Why, oh why, did I say that*?

"Oh, so you have dinner plans with your tea date?" Claire smiled.

"Again, I'm not sure it's a date. I mean, its dinner."

"Come now, my darling, that's a date."

Abby got up from the sofa. "I don't have time for this chit-chat. Claire, I'll call about the script. Let me know about your plans for this evening. I'm off to an appointment." She picked up her paperwork and left.

"I guess you like this girl?"

"She seems nice." Sara felt herself blush. *I really don't want to have this conversation with you, Claire.*

"I'm sure you'll find out more after your dinner." Claire stood up. "I have some calls to make and I have an engagement this evening, darling, so unless you have anything else for me?"

"No, I think that's it for now." Sara gathered her papers.

"Perfect. I'll see you later."

"Great." Sara went downstairs to her office. *Guess she has another date with Claudine.* Sara sat down at her desk. *Why does that piss me off?*

Claire wasn't at the brownstone Friday.

"She probably stayed with Claudine," Chloe said. She had stopped by Sara's apartment on her way from a photoshoot.

Sara was in the bathroom changing for dinner. "I guess. Abby called for some information and when I asked where Claire was, she just said she had things to take care of and that I wouldn't hear from her over the weekend."

"Maybe they went away."

"Maybe. Abby said Claire would be back on Monday." Sara came out of the bathroom buttoning up her blouse. "Do I look alright?"

Chloe turned to look at her. "Fine. Nice jeans, nice blouse. Wear those boots I got for you."

"Okay." Sara went to the closet for the boots.

"I'm also going to put a little makeup on you."

"Why?" Sara asked, returning with the boots.

"To highlight your natural beauty."

"Suppose I don't want to highlight my natural beauty?"

"Humor me, okay?"

"Fine." Sara sat on the chair Chloe brought over from the kitchen. A few minutes later she was done and Sara looked in the mirror. "Not bad, not too much."

Chloe packed up her case. "Told you. Look, I've got to run. I'm meeting Kate at seven." She kissed Sara on the cheek. "Have fun and call me tomorrow."

"I will, and thanks," Sara called after her. She finished getting ready and walked to the restaurant. It was a lovely fall evening and the restaurant was a few short blocks from her apartment. Lisa was already there when Sara arrived.

"Glad you could make it," Lisa said as Sara sat down.

"Me too. Thanks for calling."

"Have you had a busy week?"

"Not too bad."

"Good. I wanted to get together this week since next week will be busy." Lisa said as she adjusted the silverware in front of her.

The waiter approached and handed them their menus.

"What's going on next week?" Sara asked once they had ordered.

"Some papers are due and I have some exams to take."

"Practicing on any of your nieces or nephews?" Sara laughed.

"Ha, ha. Very funny."

"Yes, I think it's funny. Although I think once you become a dentist, your sister will be bugging you to work on the kids for free." Sara took a sip of water.

"What did I say? Only in emergency situations." Lisa shook her head.

They spent the rest of the evening enjoying their conversation and the meal. When they left the restaurant, they walked until Sara realized they were standing in front of her apartment building.

"Oh, wow, this is me," Sara said looking up at the building. She turned back to Lisa who was now standing very close to her.

Lisa reached out and touched Sara's face. She leaned in and they began to kiss. Slowly stopping the kiss, Lisa whispered in her ear. "How about I come up with you?"

Sara backed away. "I...um...I don't think so, Lisa."

"I'm sorry. I didn't mean to assume—"

"No, I'm sorry. I'd like to take things a little slow."

"Okay, I can do that." Lisa nodded.

"I hope that's alright?"

"Yes, it's fine." Lisa kissed Sara on the cheek. "I'll call you next week and see if we can work something out once I come up for air."

"I'd like that."

Lisa waved down a passing cab. "Talk to you soon," she said as she got in.

Sara waved as the taxi drove off. "Did not see that coming and was not ready for it," Sara mumbled as she turned and went up the steps to the door.

***

As soon as Sara arrived Monday morning, Claire called and asked her to come upstairs.

"Good morning, darling," Claire said as Sara walked into the living room.

"Morning, Claire." Sara sat down on the sofa.

Mrs. Hanson brought them tea and croissants.

"Thank you, Mrs. Hanson." Claire smiled as Mrs. Hanson set the tray on the table in front of her. Mrs. Hanson nodded and returned to the kitchen.

"So, my darling, how was your date?" Claire poured the tea and handed a cup to Sara.

"It was fine, thank you." Sara added some milk and sugar to her tea. "Interesting that you asked."

"I was just asking about your weekend, darling, that's all." Claire sipped her tea.

"Ah, but you specifically asked about my date."

"That was the start of your weekend, wasn't it?"

"I guess you could say so."

"Well then, that's why I started with your date. So how was it?"

"It was fine," Sara said as she shook her head.

"Will you see her again?" Claire asked, putting her cup on the table.

"I think so. She's busy this week with exams, but she said she will call me once her schedule clears up."

"But you think you will continue to see her?"

"Yes, although I might have scared her off a little after the kiss." *Why did I say that?* Sara mentally kicked herself.

"There was a kiss, was there?" Claire smiled and nodded as she folded her arms.

"Yes. She wanted to come up." *Stop talking.*

Claire leaned forward in her chair. "Oh, so that kiss must have been something special."

"It was unexpected. I didn't quite know how to react, and then she asked if she could come up." Sara picked up her spoon and stirred her tea again.

"Did she go to your apartment with you?"

"No." Sara shook her head. "I said I'd like to take things slow."

"Take things slow. So then sleeping with her is an option?"

Sara had just picked up her cup to take a sip but quickly put it down. "Claire, I don't think this is a conversation I want to have right now."

"I'm sorry, darling. I am interested in your well-being and if this girl is of interest to you, I'd like to know."

"Why don't we leave this conversation where it is? If anything else happens regarding my well-being, I'll let you know."

"Fair enough," Claire said as she refilled her teacup. "Would you like some more?"

"No. I think I need to get back to the office. I have some calls to make."

"That's fine. I'll be leaving shortly for some engagements. I'll see you when I get back." Claire smiled.

"Alright." *Let me just get the hell out of here,* Sara thought as she hurried away.

Gail Newman

Chapter Twenty-four

SARA DIDN'T SEE MUCH of Claire for the next few days. Before she knew it, it was Thursday and she was meeting Chloe at Finley's. They ordered martinis and went over the week's events. They discussed, among other things, Sara's date with Lisa, their kiss and Lisa asking to go with Sara to her apartment, as well as her conversation with Claire. By eight o'clock, Sara decided she deserved her third martini.

"I think we've covered it all." She giggled.

"Good thing tomorrow is Friday, and hopefully an easy workday, because you're going to feel those martinis." Chloe laughed.

"What? I'm fine. I ate those cracker thingies."

"Yes, my friend, and perhaps I need to get you something a little more substantial." Chloe started looking around for their server just as a strange noise marred their conversation.

"What's that noise?" Sara asked, looking around.

"Sounds like your cell phone," Chloe said as she held up Sara's handbag. Chloe took the phone from the bag and handed it to Sara.

Sara checked the caller ID before answering. "Hello." She quickly covered the phone as she hiccupped.

"Sara, darling, it's Claire."

"It's Claire," Sara whispered to Chloe.

"Darling, I really need your help with something."

Sara sat up straighter. "What is it, Claire?"

"Can you come to the Cameron?"

"The Cameron." Sara looked at Chloe.

"Yes, please. You know the routine."

"I'll be there in a little while."

"Thanks," Claire said before the phone disconnected.

"What's going on?" Chloe asked.

"She wants me to come to the Cameron."

"I got that. Did she say why?"

"No, just that she needed help with something." Sara started to get up but swayed on her feet.

"Hold on there. I'll get a cab and take you." Chloe waved for the server to bring their bill, and then walked with Sara to the sidewalk and hailed a cab. The next thing Sara knew, they were in front of the Cameron.

"Are you going to be okay?" Chloe asked as Sara got out of the cab.

"Yes. I think the ride cleared my head."

"Call me later." Chloe closed the cab door.

"I will."

Sara made her way to the elevators and up to the twelfth floor. She hesitated a moment before knocking on the door. *Take a deep breath,* she told herself, still feeling the effects of the martinis.

"There you are," Claire said as she opened the door and motioned for Sara to come in.

"Is everything alright?" Sara made her way to the sofa and sat down.

"Of course. I just wanted some company. Were you somewhere important?"

"You just wanted some company?" Sara gave Claire a puzzled look. "I was out with Chloe having a good time. You called, I rushed over, and all you wanted was some company?"

"I'm sorry, darling. I should have asked if it was a bother for you to come." Claire handed Sara a glass of wine.

"I was enjoying martinis with Chloe." Even though she was still feeling the effects of the martinis, she took the wine from Claire.

"I don't think I've ever seen you quite like this." Claire sat down next to Sara and smiled.

"I'm fine, just a little happy." Sara giggled.

"I can see that. How about some food to go with your happy?"

"I could use a little something." Sara started to get up.

"No, you don't. I'll get it for you." Claire went to the table and brought the plates to the sofa. "Here you are, darling. Have a little bread and cheese. That will do you a world of good."

Claire put a small plate on Sara's lap, took the wine glass from her, and set it on the table in front of them.

Sara ate what was on the plate in silence. When she was finished, she placed the plate on the table and reached for the glass of wine.

"You might just want to sip that slowly." Claire patted Sara on the knee. She took the plate back to the table and added more food to it. She poured a glass of water and brought it back to Sara.

"Gee, Claire, I didn't picture you as a caregiver." Sara looked at the food and water.

"I wouldn't call this being a caregiver. I just want you to feel better." Claire smiled.

Sara picked up the glass of water, drank it, and placed the empty glass back on the table. She sat for a moment, and then picked up the glass of wine. She took a sip and then another.

"Are you sure you don't want to stick with water?" Claire asked as she began to get up.

"No. I'm fine." Sara grabbed Claire by the arm to pull her back to the sofa.

Thrown off, Claire fell, pushing Sara over and landing almost completely on top of her. "Oh my God, darling. Are you alright?" Claire looked down at Sara.

Sara began to laugh. "I always thought Abby would try to kill me, not you."

"Oh, I would never do that." Claire smiled as she began to run her hand along the side of Sara's face. Claire looked deep into Sara's eyes before leaning in and kissing her. Soft short little kisses that became deeper and longer.

Sara's head was spinning. *What's going on? I'm kissing Claire. I should stop. This is crazy. This is Claire.* Finding just enough strength, Sara managed to get her hands on Claire's shoulders and push her back.

"Claire?"

"Yes, my darling."

"Can we take this to the bedroom?"

"Absolutely." Claire leaned in and kissed Sara again. She stood up and offered Sara her hand. Sara took it and pulled herself up. They walked hand and hand into the bedroom. As they neared the bed, Claire stopped and took Sara in her arms, kissing her. Slowly they undressed and lay on the bed. Claire again gently ran her hand over the side of Sara's face. No longer able to stand the urge, Sara pulled her into a passionate kiss. She was lost in all that was Claire.

***

Why is everything white? Sara blinked. She moved to turn over and felt the sheets against her skin. *My sheets aren't this soft.* Her eyes popped open and she struggled to sit up. Lifting the sheets, she realized she was naked. She collapsed back on the pillow and quickly sat back up as she replayed the events of the previous evening in her mind. When she realized how it ended, she gasped and covered her mouth with her hand. *What the fuck! Oh, dear God. What have I done?* She was about to get up when the door opened and Claire came in holding a tray.

"Good morning, darling," Claire said as she put the tray on a table near the bed. "Can I pour you some tea?"

Sara was dumbfounded. *Tea, she's offering me tea, after we just, just...get a grip.* "Yes, thank you, that would be nice." Sara pulled the comforter around her.

Claire sat down next to her and handed her a cup. "I made it just the way you like it, sugar and milk." She smiled as she touched Sara's cheek.

"That's great, Claire, thank you." Sara wasn't sure what to do next. She tried not to drop the comforter as she sipped the tea.

Claire got up and poured a cup for herself and returned to the bed next to Sara. They sat in silence sipping their tea. Finally, Sara couldn't stand it anymore. She put her cup on the nightstand and turned to Claire.

"Claire, I'm so sorry. I have no idea what came over me." Sara's eyes filled with tears.

Claire set her cup on the nightstand and turned to face her. Claire gently wiped Sara's tears away. "Now, my darling, what happened last night was nothing short of wonderful. I certainly don't want you to be upset. I was the one who kissed you and I may have taken advantage of the fact you were a bit tipsy."

"Claire, that's just it. I knew what I was doing, and I should have stopped." Sara shook her head and looked down.

Claire cupped Sara's chin in her hand and lifted her face. "Did you want to stop?"

"No."

"Then I don't think we have anything to worry about." Claire leaned in and softly kissed her. "Now," Claire reached for her cup of tea, "why don't we just relax with our tea and then I'll order us some breakfast."

Sara was still not comfortable with the situation. "I don't know what to do with this, Claire."

"Do with what, darling?"

"With what happened. I mean, I'm your assistant. How does this affect that?"

"Yes, let's talk about that. You are my assistant, yes, but I would like to add this type of activity to our relationship."

Sara stood up, pulling the comforter up and around her as she did. "This type of activity? What the hell does that mean?"

Claire stood up and went to Sara. "I'm sorry. I didn't say that quite right. I meant that, if you like, we can continue to see each other on more than a professional level."

Sara stared at her. "I don't know, Claire. I can barely process what happened."

"That's fine. Why don't we have some breakfast? Then you can leave, think about it, and let me know."

"I think, if it's okay with you, I'd like to just get dressed and go."

"If that's what you want, darling, that's fine."

"I think so." Sara looked around the room for her clothes. She found them on a chair and went into the bathroom to dress. When she came out, the bedroom was empty. She found Claire sitting in the living room. Suddenly Sara realized it was Friday. *Shit. I forgot about work. Now what do I do?*

"Claire, if you don't mind, I'm going to go home to change before going into work."

"That's fine, darling. I spoke to Abby and told her you might be running late, or not in at all today. You don't have to go in if you don't want to."

"Shit, Claire. You didn't tell Abby, did you?"

Claire stood up, walked over, and stood in front of Sara. "This is our little secret and will continue to be unless you decide otherwise."

Sara felt herself melting with Claire so close. She leaned in and kissed Claire on the cheek.

"I have to think," Sara said before turning to leave.

***

And think she did. All weekend long, every moment, Sara thought about what had happened and the offer Claire made to see each other on more than a professional level. Chloe was working on a photoshoot all weekend, so Sara didn't have to face her. They spoke on the phone briefly, but Sara lied and told her everything was fine. She told her it was just Claire being Claire, and that Sara sat with her for a little while at the Cameron and went home.

In the middle of a sleepless night, she decided she couldn't tell Chloe what had happened. *No. I'm not ready to share that with her, even if she is my best friend. I'll tell her when I'm ready. I'll tell her when*

I decide the time is right. I'll tell her after we're both dead.

As she walked in the park Sunday afternoon, Sara decided what she wanted to do. She sat on a bench and pulled her phone from her pocket. She took several deep breaths as the phone rang.

"Hello, my darling," Claire said when she answered the phone.

"Hi, Claire. It's me."

"Yes, I know."

"Claire, I wanted to call and let you know..." Sara hesitated as she looked around.

"Yes?"

"I want to let you know that I think I might like to take you up on your offer." Sara couldn't believe what she was saying.

"Are you sure?"

"I am. I'm just not sure how we can do this."

"It's not that hard. We do what we usually do. You come to work, and we'll make the arrangements."

"Where?" Sara looked around nervously, thinking the rest of the park could hear their conversation.

"Well, we can meet at the Cameron on Thursday. You know the routine."

"The Cameron?" Sara looked at the phone. Reality set in. *I thought you were meeting Claudine Monet there. I can't say that.*

"I wasn't sure why you were at the Cameron, Claire. Is there anything I should know?"

"No, darling. It's just away time for me. I'll explain it to you at some point. If meeting at the Cameron makes you feel uncomfortable, you can come to the townhouse."

Sara was torn. *I don't know what's been going on at the Cameron, but I sure don't want Abby walking in on us at the townhouse.* "The Cameron will be fine."

"Alright. I will see you tomorrow and it will be business as usual until Thursday."

"I'll see you tomorrow."

Sara hung up and put her phone back in her pocket. "What the fuck have I just done?" She asked the pigeon that landed on the bench next to her.

Chapter Twenty-five

IT WAS BUSINESS AS usual until Sara found herself pacing her office Thursday afternoon. She had no idea what to expect since she and Claire had not discussed the situation any further. The sound of footsteps coming down the stairs caused her to quit pacing.

"Sara, a messenger will be arriving for this envelope around five o'clock. Please make sure it gets picked up." Abby handed Sara an envelope as she put her coat on.

"No problem, Abby. I'll see to it."

"Thanks. Claire has an appointment this evening, so once the envelope is picked up you can go home. I'll see you tomorrow."

"Have a good night, Abby." Sara walked to the window and watched as Abby hailed a cab and left. Moments later she heard music upstairs. Listening closely, she recognized the song as the one Claire played weeks before. Humming along, Sara started to softly sing. A few minutes passed before the intercom rang.

"Hi, Claire." Sara smiled as she answered.

"Hello, my darling. Is there anything special that you would like this evening?"

Suddenly nervous again, Sara struggled to answer. "I...I don't know, Claire. I mean whatever you want is fine with me."

"Are you sure? Something special you might want for dinner?"

"To tell you the truth, Claire, I'm a little nervous." *No sense in trying to hide it.*

"That's alright. How about I just take care of everything and you come around eight o'clock?"

"That's fine."

"Perfect, darling. I'll see you then."

Sara stared at the phone for a minute. *Okay, calm yourself. You decided you wanted to do this. Seemed like a good idea at the time.* She took a deep breath and sat down at her desk. A few minutes later the messenger picked up the envelope. *Now what?* It was four forty-five and her plans with Claire weren't until eight o'clock. She sat down and called Chloe.

"Hi there, stranger. How are you?"

"I'm fine. Sorry I haven't called but it's been crazy around here. Can you meet me for a drink?"

"Sure. Where?"

"Our good old stomping ground, Finley's."

"What time?"

"I'll leave here in a little while. Come when you can."

"I won't be too far behind you. See you in a bit."

Sara shuffled some more paperwork as she listened to the melody playing upstairs. She called up to Claire to say she was leaving, grabbed her coat, and went out the door. The air was crisp and clear as she walked down the street. Soft lights glowed inside the windows of businesses and restaurants. Breathing deeply as she walked, she calmed herself. That was, until she realized she was in front of Finley's and had to face Chloe. *Not a word,* she reminded herself. Once inside, she grabbed two bar stools and waited.

"Hey there, girlfriend." Chloe hugged Sara when she arrived. "How are you?"

"Good. I'm good." Sara smiled back.

"We've both been busy this week."

"I know. Sorry I haven't been around." Sara signaled for the bartender.

"So, what's up with Claire lately? Anything new on the mysterious adventures of her and Claudine?"

"No, all's quiet."

"Well, you know what today is, right?" Chloe winked.

"Ah, yes. That's right, it is Thursday." Sara sank a little on her barstool.

"Guess we'll have to wait and see if you get a phone call."

Shit! How am I going to get out of here? Sara panicked. *It's not like Claire is going to call since she already knows I'm coming.* Sara nodded. "Yeah. I guess we'll have to wait and see." *Okay, at some point I'll go to the bathroom, call Claire and have her call me.*

Over the next hour, they chatted about what Chloe was currently working on and her most recent dating situation.

"So, you're still seeing her. That's good." Sara smiled.

"So far, I like her. No one else has caught my attention." Chloe sipped her wine. "That reminds me. Have you seen or spoken to Lisa?"

Lisa? Wow, I forgot all about her. "No, I haven't. I've been busy and

I'm sure she has too."

"You should call her. I think she really likes you."

"I'll see. I'm not really into seeing anyone right now." *Just a small lie.*

"Why? Is everything alright?"

"Of course. I'm just hormonal lately and, along with being busy at work, I just don't feel like it." *Another lie.* "Hey, I'm going to run to the ladies' room. I'll be right back." Sara was up and gone before Chloe could answer. She made her way to the ladies' room and into a stall where she dialed Claire's number.

"Hello, my darling. Is everything alright?"

"Yes," Sara whispered.

"Why are you whispering?"

"I'm in the ladies' room. I need you to wait a few minutes and then call me to tell me to come to the Cameron."

"Darling, what's going on?"

"I'm with Chloe and I haven't told her anything. I need you to call so I can say you need me and then I can leave."

"Okay. I'll call you in a few minutes."

"Thank you." She slipped her cell phone back into her bag and returned to Chloe to continue their conversation. They had just ordered another glass of wine when Sara's phone rang. Sara pulled it from her bag, looked at it, and rolled her eyes.

"It's Claire."

"Wow." Chloe shook her head.

"Hello, Claire." She listened while Claire asked her to come to the Cameron. "That's fine. I'll be on my way in a few minutes."

"What is up with her?" Chloe asked after Sara hung up.

"The usual. She's at the Cameron and wants me to go there."

"Is Claudine standing her up again?"

"I guess. I don't know since I can't ask." *But at some point I will have to ask, again, what's going on.* "In the meantime, let's just relax and enjoy our wine." Sara raised her glass to Chloe.

A little while later they each got into cabs and went their separate ways. Minutes later, Sara found herself knocking on the door of suite 1209. Claire opened the door and Sara walked into her waiting arms.

Gail Newman

Chapter Twenty-six

FRIDAY MORNING, SARA SAT at her desk daydreaming of the night before and what a wonderful night it had been. Sara arrived to find the suite lit only by candlelight. Fragrant flowers filled vases on each table. Dinner and wine were waiting. When they finished eating, she and Claire sat on the sofa holding hands while Claire told stories of her life growing up in Australia. Storytelling and hand holding led to soft kisses and finally to Claire taking Sara's hand and leading her to the bedroom. Sara was just starting to relive that part, the feel of Claire's touch on her body, the heat of their bodies next to each other, when the ringing of the doorbell brought her back to reality. A giant bouquet greeted Sara as she opened the door.

"I have a delivery for Ms. Elliot," a voice coming from behind the flowers said.

"Yes. I'll sign for them. You can set them down right inside here." Sara stepped aside to allow the deliveryman to put the bouquet down.

"Sign here, please." He handed Sara a clipboard.

"Thank you." She handed the clipboard back to him before closing the door and turning to look at the bouquet. *Wonder who these are from?*

She peeked through the flowers for a card. When she found no card, she picked them up and took them upstairs to the living room where she placed them on the cocktail table. As she turned to go back to her office, she heard Claire come down the stairs from her bedroom.

"Good morning, my darling," Claire said as she walked over to Sara and placed a soft kiss on her cheek. "Thank you for a wonderful evening."

"Thank you." Sara smiled and she felt herself begin to blush.

Claire stepped back and admired the flowers. "What do we have here?"

"Not sure. They were just delivered," Sara answered as she touched one of the flower petals. "They are beautiful."

"Let's see if there's a card." Claire picked her way around the top of the bouquet until she found a small white envelope. She opened it and read what was on the card. She put the card back in the envelope and stuck it back in the bouquet. She turned away and sat down on the sofa.

Sara looked at the flowers before going to stand in front of Claire.

"So, who are they from?"

Before Claire could answer, they heard the door open and Abby talking on the phone as she came in and up the stairs.

"You are not going to believe what happened," Abby said as she came into the living room.

"What is it?" Claire asked.

"That interview we had scheduled for Monday has been changed to today. In an hour, Claire. You need to get ready. We need to leave in fifteen minutes if we are going to get through traffic."

"Oh, bloody hell. Come with me and help me get ready," Claire said as she rose from the sofa.

Abby turned to Sara. "Sara, do me a favor. Grab the file about this interview I gave you yesterday. I'll need to go over it with Claire. Please call and let us know when the car arrives. We have to move fast."

Abby followed Claire up to the bedroom. Sara hesitated a moment and then looked for the card in the flowers. She pulled it out and looked at the envelope. There was a "C" written on it. Quickly, she opened the envelope and read the card. "I miss you." It was signed "Claude." *Claude? What the fuck?*

She slid the card back in the envelope and replaced it in the bouquet. She hurried down the stairs and located the file just as the car pulled up. She called Abby to let her know the car was there. A few minutes later Claire and Abby were out the door.

Sara sat down at her desk. *What's going on? Obviously something was, or is, going on with Claire and Claudine, but is it still? And how do I fit into all this?* Sara shook her head. *How can I ask Claire about Claudine if I'm not supposed to know?*

Claire and Abby didn't return to the townhouse by the time Sara left for the day. She spent the weekend torturing herself over Claire and Claudine. Somehow, someway, she had to figure out what was going on.

Chapter Twenty-seven

THE NEXT FEW WEEKS flew by. The passion of Sara and Claire's Thursday night rendezvous grew more intense. Sara was so enamored with Claire that she stopped thinking there could possibly be anything going on with Claudine, or anyone else for that matter. When she was with Claire, nothing else mattered. She lied to Chloe about what she was doing on Thursday nights, telling her she was taking a screenwriting class at a local school. Nothing would stand in the way of her time with Claire.

One Tuesday morning when she arrived at work, a note from Claire was on her desk. Sara thought it would be one of the little notes Claire had started leaving for her before their Thursday nights. The notes always said the same thing, "the usual place." Sara would hum the song for hours after reading the note. This note, however, asked her to come up to the living room when she arrived. After putting her things away, she hurried up the staircase to find Claire and Abby sitting in the living room.

"Good morning, my darling." Claire smiled at Sara as she entered the room.

"Morning, Claire. Morning, Abby." Sara greeted them as she walked to a chair and sat down.

"Hello, Sara," Abby said.

"Sara, darling, Abby and I need to speak to you about something." Sara looked at them. "What is it?"

"Darling, I have an event I must attend on Thursday evening. Abby can't go with me and I was wondering if you would be able to go?"

Thursday? Our Thursday? "I guess. I mean, yes, I can."

"Sorry for the short notice, but I just can't make it," Abby said as she stood up. "Claire will tell you the details and if you need more information, you can ask me. I'm off. I'll be back later." She picked up her coat and some paperwork and left.

Sara and Claire sat in silence until they heard the front door close.

"I know what you're thinking, my darling, but this really can't be helped." Claire patted the cushion next to her.

"It's fine, Claire. I know there are going to be times like this, especially once your next project starts." Sara sat down next to her.

Claire took Sara's hand. "That's why we shouldn't just limit ourselves to Thursdays. I was thinking that perhaps we should open our affair to being more of a relationship. What do you think?'

"Claire, I don't know what to say. Are you saying that maybe we should be out in the open and date?"

Claire stood up and walked a few steps. She turned to look at Sara. "I don't know if I'm ready to go out in public quite yet. I was thinking more along the lines of you staying here overnight, or perhaps I could come to your apartment?"

"I think coming to my apartment might cause a ruckus in my building. I'm sure someone would recognize you. It might be better if we thought of a way to stay here."

"We can do that." Claire returned to the sofa and sat next to Sara. "We will go to the event on Thursday, and then we can make plans for Friday or Saturday night, whichever you prefer. You can come here, and I'll cook dinner."

"You did promise to cook me dinner some time." Sara laughed.

"Yes, I did. Shall we plan on it?"

"That sounds perfect."

They sat in silence for a few minutes, smiling at each other.

"What is the event on Thursday?" Sara asked.

"It's a cocktail reception for a friend who has an art show opening. The opening is in Paris and this reception is for his friends in New York who won't be able to make it. Some of his works will be on display before they get sent to Paris. Oh, I wish I could take you to Paris for the opening. I told you I would take you there someday."

"You did. That and dinner. So now that I'm getting dinner, I'll have to hold you to Paris." Sara shook her finger at Claire.

Claire grabbed Sara's hand and kissed it. "Now, there will be some press at this event and a red-carpet entrance."

"I'd like to avoid both the press and red-carpet, so I'll meet you inside." Sara rose from the sofa.

"That will be perfect. I like to have Abby with me at these types of things because she always knows how to move me along when I get stuck speaking to someone too long."

"Is that what you would like me to do as well?"

"Yes, darling. Usually I give Abby a slight wink if I need to get away, but she is quite good at spotting the issue beforehand. If she doesn't want me to speak to someone, she comes up to me and whispers something in my ear and I can tell the person I need to go."

"What does she whisper?"

"Sometimes a line from one of my movies or a lyric from a song."

"I'll try and come up with something. Until then, I need to get down to the office. What should I wear Thursday?"

Claire walked over to Sara and gently caressed her face. "Why don't I have something sent here for you to wear? That way we can leave directly from here and you won't have to go home."

"You don't have to—"

Claire stopped her words with a kiss. "I want to," she said, her lips still close to Sara's.

Sara felt her body melting.

"Okay. That's fine, but if I don't go right now, I'm not going to be able to control myself."

"Why don't we save that for the weekend?" Claire brushed her lips over Sara's.

"That's it. I'm going downstairs." Sara spun on her heels and walked away. She turned back to smile at Claire and then went down the stairs.

Gail Newman

Chapter Twenty-eight

THURSDAY ARRIVED, AND SARA nervously awaited the arrival of her outfit. *What could Claire possibly pick out for me? I'm just supposed to be in the background, so why bother? Well, I might not always know what to wear.*

A little after noon the doorbell rang and Sara accepted a large box from the delivery person. She carried it into her office and set it on the chair. Sara worried about telling Chloe about the event but finally, on Wednesday, she called and told her. Chloe offered to do Sara's hair and makeup, but Sara assured her it wouldn't be necessary.

"Are you sure?" Chloe asked.

"Thanks. I really appreciate it but I'm only there to run interference if needed."

"Alright. Have a good time. Let's get together soon. I've missed you."

"I miss you too. I'll call you next week. I'm on call for Claire this weekend, so I don't want to make any plans I can't keep."

It was a small lie, Sara told herself, and as soon as she and Claire decided where to take their relationship, Chloe would be the first to know. For now, Sara was looking forward to whichever night she and Claire decided on for this weekend.

Three o'clock came and went and finally, at three-thirty, Sara heard a car pull up. She looked out the window to see Claire emerge from the car along with her hair and make-up stylists. Sara opened the door for them.

"Hello, my darling," Claire said as she breezed in. "You remember Jon-Paul and Madeline?"

"Yes. Hello," Sara said as she stepped out of the way.

"Darling, we are going upstairs so I can take my shower and they can get started on my hair and make-up. Why don't you come up in an hour? They can do yours if you like and then we'll get dressed. The car will be here at six o'clock."

"That sounds good."

"Wonderful." Claire smiled as she turned and led them up the stairs.

Hair and make-up? The thought made Sara uncomfortable. After all, she had only allowed Chloe to do that for her one time and she had turned down her help for this event. *I won't let them do anything I don't want.* She settled down at her desk and worked until four-thirty.

Here we go. Sara steadied herself as she climbed the stairs carrying the box. She found Claire seated in front of the large vanity mirror in the bathroom as Jon-Paul finished her hair. He had done it just the way Sara loved it, long with soft waves.

Claire smiled when she saw Sara in the mirror. "Alright, my darling, it's your turn. Jon-Paul is going to give you a soft blow out just the way you had it the night of the awards ceremony. I've already described it to him." Claire got up from the chair and walked over to Sara and touched her arm. "I know you don't want anything too elaborate. I loved the way you looked that night, so I thought that's what you would be most comfortable with."

Sara smiled and nodded. "Thank you, Claire."

Claire turned to Jon-Paul. "She's all yours."

After he washed her hair, Sara sat in the chair and Jon-Paul went to work. He checked with Sara as he did, making sure he was doing exactly what she wanted. Claire sat in another chair and offered some comments as Madeline did her make-up. Once they were done, Claire went to the bedroom with Jon-Paul to dress while Sara stayed with Madeline for her make-up. Claire had instructed her to do Sara's make-up exactly as Chloe had. They finished just as Claire came back to check on them. She looked stunning in a long-sleeved, gold dress.

"You look beautiful," Sara said as she turned in the chair to look at her.

"Thank you, my darling. I see you're about finished."

"We are," Madeline said.

"Wonderful. Jon-Paul and I opened the box and laid out the clothes for you. When you're ready, come into the bedroom and get dressed," Claire said as she left the bathroom.

A few minutes later, with her hair and make-up done, Sara went into the bedroom. A beautiful black velvet tuxedo lay on the bed. Sara gasped when she saw it. Claire came and stood next to her.

"You like it?"

"Oh, Claire, it's beautiful."

"Now you know," Claire whispered. "It has a slightly plunging neckline and you don't wear a bra under it. Madeline will help you with that. You know, to hold the girls in place."

"I thought I was to be inconspicuous," Sara said with a nervous laugh.

"You will be, my darling. Elegantly inconspicuous. Now, get dressed and I'll see you in the living room." Claire smiled as she turned and left.

Sara picked up the jacket and held it close to her chest. A second later, Madeline appeared to help her dress.

A little while later, Sara entered the living room where Claire sat waiting. "You look beautiful, my darling." Claire stood up from the sofa and walked to Sara.

"Thank you." Sara curtsied. "It's so beautiful, Claire. I can't thank you enough. I will tell you one thing." Sara leaned in close to Claire. "You were right, the girls aren't going anywhere."

"I told you," Claire said as she gave a playful tug to the jacket.

***

Moments later, they sat holding hands in the back of the town car on the way to the opening.

"My darling, are you comfortable arriving with me, or do you want the car to drop you off first?" Claire asked as the car drew closer to its destination.

"What would Abby do?"

"Abby? Well, Abby always stays close by, so she arrives with me. But this is about what you are comfortable with. I don't think there will be a lot of press but there might be some."

"I'll go with you."

"Perfect." Claire opened the glass between them and the driver. "Ted, Ms. Burton will be arriving with me."

"Alright, Ms. Elliot. We're about two minutes out."

"Thank you," Claire said as she closed the glass. She turned to Sara. "Nervous?"

"Yes. What should I do when we get there?"

"I'll get out first, with Ted's help. Then he'll help you out and you walk along with me."

"You mean, like next to you? Shouldn't I walk a few steps behind?"

"Not at all. You stay with me. Once we're inside, we might get separated by people chatting us up. How would you like me to introduce you? I don't want to make a mistake like last time."

"Not as a screenwriter or a work in progress," Sara said. "I think as your assistant would be best. How do you introduce Abby?"

"Abby." Claire tapped her chin as she thought for a moment. "Abby's been around so long that people recognize her. In situations where people don't know her, she is my agent or publicist, whichever word comes to mind."

"I think assistant will work."

The car slowed and then stopped in front of the gallery. Ted came around and opened the door. Taking Ted's hand, Claire got out of the car and waited for Sara. A small group of fans and photographers stood off to the side calling Claire's name as they walked inside. Upon entering, they were each handed a glass of champagne. People milled about looking at the exhibited artwork.

"Claire. So glad you could make it," a man said as he joined them.

"William, darling, how wonderful to see you." Claire kissed him on the cheek.

"It's always wonderful to see you."

"William, let me introduce you to Sara." Claire smiled at Sara.

"It's nice to meet you, Sara." William extended his hand.

"It's nice to meet you too," Sara said as she shook his hand.

"Ladies, you'll have to forgive me, but I must mingle. Please, relax and enjoy yourselves, and once things calm down, Claire, I'll be back to chat."

"Go, William. We'll be just fine." Claire raised her glass as she turned her attention back to Sara. "Shall we take a look around?"

"I'd love to." Sara smiled.

They made their way around the room, stopping to look at each piece and discussing what they saw. Other guests said hello to Claire as they passed. While they stood admiring one of the pieces of art, a familiar face joined them.

"Peter, how are you?" Claire asked as she kissed him on the cheek.

"Never better, Claire. How good it is to see you."

"Peter, you remember Sara." Claire turned to look at Sara.

"Of course, I do. How are you, Sara? And more importantly, how is the screenplay coming?"

Sara blushed. "I'm well, thank you. As for the writing, I haven't had much of a chance to work on it."

They were interrupted by a woman whispering in Claire's ear.

"Would you excuse me for a moment?" Claire asked as she walked a few steps away with the woman.

Sara strained to keep an eye on Claire but was unable to as Peter continued their conversation as though they hadn't been interrupted.

"What's stopping you?"

"I'm not really sure. Lack of time, lack of incentive. Sometimes I wonder why I even started it or if I should continue."

Peter looked at her for a moment. "There's something about you, Sara. I'm not quite sure what it is, but there is something about you that tells me you can be good. Why don't you look at what you've written and then give me a call? I'd be happy to look at it, even if it's just to tell you I was wrong." He smiled. "Somehow, I don't think that will be the case."

"Thank you, Peter. I might take you up on that offer." They chatted a few more moments before Peter was called away to another conversation.

Sara looked around the room. Claire was nowhere in sight. A waiter passed her and handed her another glass of champagne. She walked through the crowd scanning the faces for Claire. As she turned the corner into another section of the gallery, she saw her. Claire was on the other side of the room. It seemed she was having a deep conversation with someone. Sara couldn't see who she was speaking with because of the people between them.

Maneuvering herself through the crowd, she found a spot where she might get a glimpse of who Claire was speaking to. Just as the crowd parted, Sara saw Claire release someone's hand and walk away. Sara struggled to see who it was, but again, her view was blocked by the crowd. By the time the view was cleared, Claire was gone. Sara spied another waiter and downed her champagne, placed the empty glass on the tray, and picked up another before the waiter had a chance to stop. She felt a hand on her shoulder and turned to face Claire.

"There you are, darling." Claire smiled at her.

"Yes, here I am, but where have you been?" Sara shot back.

"Why, chatting with some people. What's wrong, darling? Why are you annoyed?"

Shit. What do I say? I think I know what I saw but suppose I'm wrong. Maybe I'm just being silly. Come up with something. "I thought I saw you deep in conversation with someone," Sara said, choosing honesty.

"Really? Well, some of those conversations can start to go that way. I usually try and break away from those quickly at these events and then I drift from one person to the next, making light conversation and seeing old friends."

Old friends? Could one of them have been Claudine? I can't ask that. How would I know if Claudine had been here? Stop making yourself crazy. "Anyone I should meet?" Sara asked.

"Why don't we take a turn around the room and I'll introduce you to anyone I know." Claire linked her arm through Sara's as they began to walk. "Then, let's go back to the house," she whispered. Claire's soft breath against her ear caused tingling up and down Sara's spine.

"Okay." She couldn't manage to say anything else.

***

A few hours later they were back in the car and soon arrived at the townhouse. In the living room, Sara sat on the sofa while Claire retrieved a bottle of wine and two glasses from the kitchen. After pouring them each a glass, Claire sat down next to Sara.

"So, my darling, did you enjoy the evening?"

"Yes, it was nice." Sara momentarily flashed back to Claire releasing someone's hand. She shook off the thought.

"You seem preoccupied. Is everything alright?" Claire touched Sara's hand.

"Yes. I'm sorry. I was rethinking the events of the evening."

"Good. I hope you would tell me if something was wrong."

"I would." Sara managed a small smile to reassure Claire.

"Now, if I don't get these shoes off, my feet will swell." Claire slipped her heels off. She picked up her wine glass and turned to Sara as she put her legs under her on the sofa.

"Do get comfortable, darling, and let's chat awhile." Claire patted the sofa.

Claire took Sara's glass from her and watched as Sara slid her shoes off.

Claire smiled. "That's better. So, tell me about your name. It's a beautiful name. So many powerful women throughout history named Sara. Are you named for someone from the past? Or someone from your family?"

Sara laughed. "Actually, it's from a song."

Claire's eyes widened. "Really? A song?"

"Yes, but don't get too excited. It's not historical or anything like that." Sara took a sip of wine.

"Tell me."

"My mother loves Stevie Nicks and I am named for her song 'Sara.'"

Claire shook her head as a smile grew on her face.

"What?"

"It's so interesting. I'm named after a song as well."

"Really?"

"Yes. My mother loved 'Claire de Lune' by Claude Debussy. It's from a suite whose name escapes me." Claire waved her hand dismissively.

"It's a beautiful song. I can play it on the piano."

"Really, darling? You play the piano?"

Sara laughed again. "It's been a while but yes, I took lessons as a child. I have been known to sit and play when there is a piano available. I don't usually play if there are a lot of people around. Never know when I might hit a wrong note."

"I would love to hear you sometime. Maybe I can arrange a private showing." Claire reached for the wine bottle and refilled both their glasses.

"Just don't go and rent anything. I'd hate to disappoint you."

Claire took Sara's hand. "I don't think you could ever disappoint me. What other interests do you have?"

Sara thought for a moment. "You know I have an interest in writing, which for some reason I can't seem to get out of my own way and do."

"Yes, there is that." Claire laughed lightly.

"I would like to travel more."

"But you do get to travel."

"I do, but I don't usually get to see much more than the inside of a trailer or a movie set. Most of the scenery flies by on the way to or from the airport."

"We'll have to change that." Claire slapped her hand on her thigh. "At our next location, we'll make time do some sightseeing."

"Really, Claire?"

Claire stood up and walked a few feet away before turning around to look at Sara. "I have a better idea. Why don't we go away together?"

"What?" Sara gave Claire a puzzled look.

"Let's go away together. Anywhere you want, my darling."

Sara stood up and went to Claire. "I don't know about that."

"Darling, it will be wonderful. Please, give it some thought. You and me somewhere fabulous, all alone together." Claire looked deep into Sara's eyes.

"What about Abby?" Sara shook her head.

"What's Abby got to do with anything?"

"Abby has something to do with everything." Sara turned away and went back to the sofa. "She doesn't like me. Don't you think she'll wonder why the two of us are going away together? I don't think we should do it, Claire."

Claire sat next to Sara and took her hands. "I'll handle everything with Abby. You don't have to worry about that."

"I don't know."

Claire leaned over and began to kiss the side of Sara's face, softly whispering, "Not to worry, darling. I'll take care of it."

"I...I'll think...about it."

"You do that," Claire answered as she began to unbutton Sara's jacket. When she undid the last one, she slowly pushed the jacket open and drew Sara closer. She leaned in and began to kiss Sara's neck and shoulders.

Sara felt Claire's body rise as she finally reached her lips. Wrapping her arms around Claire their kisses became more intense.

After a few moments, Claire whispered, "Come upstairs with me."

"Yes," Sara whispered back.

Holding hands, they climbed the stairs together. When they reached the bedroom, they slowly undressed each other and laid down on the bed.

Their lovemaking was tender and passionate. Afterwards, they lay in each other's arms, Sara softly whispered, "I love you." Claire returned the sentiment with only a kiss.

Chapter Twenty-nine

SARA LEFT THE TOWNHOUSE in the early morning hours in order to avoid being discovered by Abby. The note she left for Claire read, *I'm ready to go anywhere with you*.

After she showered and put on clean clothes, Sara couldn't resist the temptation to sneak back into the townhouse to see Claire for one more moment before the workday started. On a typical morning, she arrived at the townhouse between eight-thirty and nine, but it was before seven when she quietly let herself back in. As she climbed the stairs, she heard voices in the living room. She stopped to listen as she got close to the top of the stairs.

"Are you sure about all this?" She heard someone ask.

"Of course I am."

Okay, that was Claire. But who is she talking to?

"I hope you are, because if you're not..."

That's Abby. I wonder what they're talking about.

"Nothing is going to happen," Claire said.

"Look, Claire, I hope that's the case, but if she finds out that this is all a ruse to get her, how do you think she's going to feel?"

"I hope she'll think that I went to a lot of trouble."

"No. I think you're asking for a lot of trouble. Once Sara finds out that you've been playing her this whole time..."

What the fuck did she just say? Sara's head started to spin.

"Sara is not going to find out. I can handle this."

"How? Are you going to keep letting her think this is all happening by magic? Don't you think at some point she's going to realize that you've orchestrated everything?"

Claudine and the Cameron were all made up? I'm about to find out. Sara went up the last step and into the room.

"Is that the truth, Claire? Is this all some movie you made up?" Sara's face turned red.

Claire turned, a startled look on her face. "My darling, when did you get here? I didn't hear you come in." Claire rushed over to her.

"Apparently not." Sara began to cry. "Is it true, Claire? Did you play me like some sort of game?"

Claire turned to look at Abby.

"That's my cue. I'll be in the kitchen." Abby turned and left the room.

"Please come sit so we can talk." Claire started to take Sara's arm.

"No, Claire." Sara pulled away. "I can't believe this. What a fool I've been. I never thought—"

"Sara, please, just come sit down. I have so much to explain."

"No. No, you leave me alone," Sara screamed. "I thought this was happening between us. But you've been planning it all along. I don't know what to believe anymore. Now the pieces make sense. Those unexplained nights at the Cameron, making me think there was something going on with Claudine."

"Claudine? Sara, what are you talking about?" Again, Claire moved close to her.

"You know exactly what I'm talking about. Making me think you were with her. For what? So that I would get jealous?"

"Sara, please let me explain," Claire pleaded.

"I told you I loved you. What a fool I am." Sara ran down the stairs, grabbed her jacket and bag, and went out the door. Once on the street, she started walking toward Chloe's apartment. She pulled out her cell phone and called her. All she could stammer was that she was on her way. Chloe was waiting on the steps for her as she walked up. Sara collapsed in tears in Chloe's arms.

***

For two days, between bouts of hysterical crying, Sara tried to tell Chloe what happened. On the third day, she sat on the floor with a cup of tea and told Chloe everything. "I'm sorry, Chloe. I should have told you from the start. You would have stopped me from making a fool out of myself."

"Look, Sara, what happened has happened. I don't know if anything I could have said would have been the right thing."

"No, you would have figured out that I was being played." Sara started to cry again.

Chloe placed another box of tissues in front of her. "First of all, wow, I didn't think you had any moisture left in you to make tears. You have barely eaten or drunk anything. Second, I doubt that you would have believed me if I thought that Claire was playing you. You'd be mad at me for even suggesting it, and who knows, maybe we wouldn't be friends anymore."

"Oh God, Chloe, don't say that. I could never not want you as my friend. You're my best friend."

"Sara, I know that. But many a friendship has been ruined over love."

"Love? Please don't say that word. I can't believe I told her that I loved her." Sara shook her head.

"You said it because you meant it." Chloe got up to get the teapot and poured more tea in both their cups.

"She didn't say it back."

"Maybe she wasn't ready."

"Wasn't ready?" Sara's voice rose. "She was after me. If she didn't think she loved me or was going to love me, why did she bother?"

"I guess that's up to Claire to explain."

"No. I don't think so. I never want to see or speak to her again," Sara said through gritted teeth.

"Well, someone is going to have to." Chloe picked up Sara's cell phone. "There must be like, I don't know, a hundred voice mails from her along with dozens of text messages."

"I don't care. I'll delete them all."

"You can do whatever you want when you are ready. But since she has my number, she called and texted me, so I called her and told her you were here and okay."

"What the fuck, Chloe? Why did you do that?"

"Because she was frantic when she couldn't get hold of you. She called me, so I responded."

"Frantic, my ass. She's just trying to do damage control. She probably thinks I'll tell my story to the press." Sara held her head in her hands.

"Think what you want, but the Claire I spoke to was genuinely concerned about you."

"Careful, she tells a good story." Sara looked up and laughed sarcastically.

"Look, whatever. I did what I did. She knows you're okay."

"Okay?" Sara looked at Chloe. "I'll never be okay again."

The next day, Sara decided to go home. On the way, she stopped at the local cell phone store and bought a new phone with a new number. She then deleted all the phone and text messages from Claire. Before the store clerk deactivated her old cell phone, Sara sent one last text to Claire. *Stop.*

Gail Newman

Chapter Thirty

OVER THE NEXT WEEK, Sara perused job websites for something of interest. She kept telling herself that the rent money wasn't going to grow on the tree outside her window. One day late in the week, the doorbell ringing roused her from her seat. Through the intercom, the postal worker told her that she had a certified letter requiring her signature. After signing for it, she returned to her apartment.

Um, no return address, she noticed as she sliced the envelope open with a letter opener. The envelope held a folded piece of paper as well as another small envelope. As she removed the paper, she realized it was a hand-written note from Claire. Her first instinct was to rip it up, but her curiosity got the best of her.

My darling,

Words cannot express my sorrow at hurting you. I will never forgive myself. I hope that one day you will give me the chance to explain. I won't say any more, as I fear you may not read this at all or will stop reading if I go on. Please accept what I have enclosed in this envelope. I hope it might be of help in the immediate future.

Claire

Sara began to cry but took a deep breath and willed the tears to stop. "Oh no you don't. I'm done crying over you." She debated not opening the second envelope but finally sliced it open. Inside was a check for five thousand dollars. Sara sat looking at the check. *What the fuck? Is she trying to buy me off?* She picked up the phone and called Chloe.

"Look, Sara, five thousand dollars wouldn't shut anyone up if they wanted to sell this story. The press would pay a lot more than that for the scoop you have."

"Scoop? What scoop? I don't have a scoop."

"She said it was for the immediate future, right?"

"Yes."

"Then I think she knows you have rent and bills that need to be paid. You don't have a job anymore, and you can't collect unemployment." Chloe started to laugh.

"What's so funny?" Sara asked, slightly annoyed.

"I was just thinking of what category you would register under with unemployment as to why you left your job. Wait, I know, sexual harassment. No. I think you need a lawyer for that one."

"Thanks, Chloe. You always know how to make me feel better." Sara shook her head as she looked at the phone.

"Hold onto that check until you decide what you want to do with it. Want to have a drink tonight?"

"I'm not sure. Can I call you later? I'm looking for a job."

"While you're doing that, why don't you check to see if there are any writing courses you might be interested in?"

"Why in the world would you say that?" Sara put her hand over her eyes.

"Look, you have a little breathing room with this check. You should occupy your time. It seems like a perfect opportunity to do what you've been threatening to do for the longest time and write something or take a class about writing."

Sara thought for a moment before answering. "You might actually have a brilliant idea. I could take a course in the evening, get a job during the day, and maybe, just maybe, move myself in the right direction."

"Brilliant, that's me. I have to go. Call me later and let me know if you want to grab a drink, or I'll call you tomorrow."

"I will. Bye."

Sara left the job listing site she was on and turned her research to writing classes. After looking at numerous sites, she decided to register for an evening class at a local university. It was two nights a week and covered screenwriting as well as touching on playwriting. Feeling better about herself, she went back to the job search. After poring over them for hours, she finally found a posting for help at a small bookstore. She decided to check it out the next morning.

Not wanting to miss an opportunity, Sara was waiting at the bookstore when it opened at nine o'clock. After meeting with the owner, she was given the job. She would assist the owner in stocking the shelves, waiting on customers, and any light errands that needed to be run. Her hours would be from nine o'clock to three o'clock, Monday through Friday, and an occasional Saturday if needed.

It's perfect. I can work, take my classes, and find time to write. Anything to take my mind off where it wants to go.

Chapter Thirty-one

SARA AND CHLOE SAT in silence on a bench in the park, sipping hot chocolate, and watching the snow fall. It was February, and after the hustle and bustle of the holiday season, the city belonged to the locals. Things were returning to a somewhat normal routine for Sara with her work at the bookstore and her classes. She hadn't heard from Claire, and the few times Chloe had brought up the subject, Sara immediately shut her down. The quiet was broken by the sound of laughter as two girls bundled up for the cold were passing by. One of them stopped in front of Sara.

"Sara?" She asked as she dropped the scarf that covered her mouth.

"Lisa. Hi."

"Hi. It's been a long time. How are you?"

"I'm good. How about you?"

"I'm fine, thanks. Still in dental school. By the way, this is my sister Anne. Anne, this is Sara."

"Hi, Sara. It's nice to meet you." Anne uncovered her face and greeted Sara with a smile.

"Nice to meet you too. This is my friend, Chloe."

"Hi," Chloe said with a wave.

"We're heading off to see a show. Anne's been here for the weekend and is leaving tomorrow."

"Perfect thing to do on this cold day," Sara said.

"How about I give you a call this week and maybe we can have dinner and catch up?" Lisa began to wrap the scarf back around her face.

"That sounds good, but I'll call you since I have a new phone number."

"I'll look forward to it. Nice to see you both." With that, Lisa linked arms with her sister and they walked off.

"So?" Chloe asked.

"So, what?" Sara looked at her.

"So, are you going to call her or are you going to blow her off again?"

"I didn't blow her off. I was otherwise engaged at the time."

"So, are you going to call her this time?"

"Yes, Chloe, I'm going to call her this time."

"I'll believe it when I see it." Chloe stood up. "Come on. I can't feel my feet any longer and I think it's time for lunch and something stronger than hot chocolate."

"Sounds good to me. And, yes, I am going to call her."

"Fine. Call her, don't call her. I don't care."

Bumping her shoulder as they started to walk, Sara laughed. "Of course you care what I do. You have a vested interest in my life. That's what best friends are for."

"I'll be fully there once I get warm." Chloe laughed and linked her arm through Sara's.

***

During a quiet period at the bookstore on Wednesday, Sara called Lisa and they decided to meet for dinner Friday night. Sara was the first to arrive and, a few minutes later, Lisa was shown to the table.

"Hi, there," she said as she sat down.

"Hi. Is it cold enough for you?"

"It feels good. I like the cold weather."

The waiter appeared and took their drink orders.

Settling back into the conversation, Lisa asked, "So how have you been? I have to apologize for not getting in touch with you. After I saw you in the fall, things got busy with school, then the holidays, and everything else in life."

"That's okay. I had a lot going on at the time as well and things are finally calming down."

"Busy at work?"

"Sort of. I'm not working at the same job I was the last time you saw me." Sara willed the flashback from her mind.

"What? No more traveling with the movie star?"

"No. I'm currently working at a bookstore and taking some writing classes. Very low key compared to before."

"As long as you're happy." Lisa smiled.

"I am for now. I guess I'll see where it takes me."

"Maybe someday you'll tell me who the movie star was."

"I don't know about that. I think there might be some sort of confidentiality clause or something." Sara was saved from saying more when the waiter brought their drinks. "How is school going?"

"It's good. I'm starting to see the light at the end of the tunnel."

"So, then, you'll get to practice on the nieces and nephews." Sara laughed.

"Right? I'm glad you remembered."

"Of course. How are they all doing?"

"Everyone's good. I'd love for you to meet them sometime. You met my sister in the park the other day."

Whoa. Meet the family? The fact that I'm even here is a lot for me. "Maybe some time." Sara shifted in her seat and looked away from Lisa.

"I'm sorry, Sara. I seem to be getting ahead of myself. I...well I thought that we could continue to see each other if that is something you'd be interested in?"

Sara thought for a moment before she answered. "Can we take things slow and see how it goes? You know, like maybe another dinner and a movie."

"I can do that." Lisa smiled.

"Okay, let's start with dinner tonight and go from there."

"To tonight." Lisa raised her glass.

"To tonight." Sara clicked her glass against Lisa's.

Gail Newman

Chapter Thirty-two

ONE NIGHT, AFTER AN especially enjoyable class, Sara dug out the screenplay she had been working on for years. After she made a cup of tea, she took the worn pages clipped together by a giant paperclip and sat by the window to read it. Within a few minutes, she got up and threw the papers in the trash bin. She circled the room a few times before sitting down in front of her computer. She opened a new file and began typing away.

Before she knew it, light was coming through the window. Sitting back, she looked out the window and watched as the light grew brighter. She smiled at the thought of a new day and what she hoped she had accomplished overnight. She flipped the switch on the printer and waited as page after page churned out of the machine. When it stopped, she took the pages and stacked them in a neat pile. Looking at the time, she realized she had just enough time to catch a little sleep before she had to be at work.

That afternoon she sat by the window to read what she had written. Soon she was back at her computer, breaking for only a few minutes to print pages and add them to the stack. When her stomach growled, she stopped long enough to make a sandwich. She continued to write and revise until after midnight when she decided she needed to sleep. She continued this routine for the next two days until she typed the words "The End." She stood up and stretched before she went to the kitchen and poured herself a glass of wine. Back in front of the computer, she once again hit the print button. As the pages started to print, she held up her glass of wine.

"To me," she said as she took a sip.

***

"So, what are you planning to do with it?" Chloe asked Sara later that week.

They were sitting in a restaurant waiting for Lisa and Chloe's girlfriend.

"I'm not quite sure yet. I guess I could show it to my writing teacher, maybe get some feedback."

"How about sending it to that guy?"

"What guy?" Sara gave Chloe a puzzled look.

"The guy Claire knew. You know, the one you went to the awards thing for."

"Chloe, how the hell did you remember that?"

"Listen, I may not remember a lot of things, but I thought he sounded cool when you told me about him." Chloe paused and took a sip of her drink. "He told you to send him your work."

Sara thought a minute. "Peter Harper. I can't do that."

"Why not?"

"Because of...you know."

"What?"

"Because of Claire," Sara whispered.

"What's she got to do with this?" Chloe threw up her hands.

"Chloe, keep your voice down."

"Why? Who's going to hear me?"

"I don't know. I mean, you know we don't talk about her."

"Okay, I get it. I don't think there's anything wrong in sending your screenplay to someone who has offered to help you." Chloe shrugged her shoulders.

"I'll think about it."

"Don't think, just do it."

"Alright, but let's stop talking about it. Lisa and Cass could show up at any minute."

"Fine. Just promise me you'll send it." Chloe pointed her finger at Sara

"I'm not promising anything." Sara laughed as she grabbed Chloe's finger.

Later that evening, Sara looked through her contacts and found an email address for Peter. She typed a short note to remind him who she was and where they had met before attaching the file and sending it off.

Chapter Thirty-three

SARA LAY AWAKE WATCHING the patterns of light as they made shapes on the window shade. It had been one week since she had sent the file off to Peter. So far there was no response. She turned over determined not to think about it anymore and go to sleep. A warm body moved close to her.

"Can't sleep?" Lisa whispered.

Sara looked over her shoulder. "Not really."

"Maybe I can help." Lisa moved closer to Sara. "I think I know just the thing." She softly began to kiss Sara's back.

Sara had resisted for a while, she finally decided she needed to move on with her life and that, for the time being, meant more of a relationship with Lisa. As she turned over to face Lisa, she allowed herself to think again as she had done before, *It's not Claire.*

A few days later, when she arrived home from work, she turned on her computer and found an email from Peter Harper. She sat and looked at it for a moment, got up and paced the room, and sat down again. She hadn't told anyone she sent the file, not even Chloe. If it wasn't the answer she hoped for, she wanted to deal with the disappointment alone. *Fine. If he doesn't like it, I'll send it to someone else. Everyone gets rejected the first time.* Taking a deep breath, she clicked on the email to open it.

"Dear Sara," it began.

"Great," she said out loud. "It's a Dear John email."

Steadying herself, she read more. It was no Dear John email. Of course, he remembered her. He liked what he read and wanted to meet with her. She read the email over and over again until she finally stood up and yelled, "Oh my God."

She sat back down and told him she could meet him anytime, anywhere. She didn't care if she had to miss work or a class to do it. When she finished typing and hit send, she sat for a moment, not sure what to do next. When she couldn't contain her excitement anymore, she grabbed her cell phone.

"Hey, what's up?" Chloe answered.

"Where are you?" Sara was pulling on her jacket.

"I'm heading home."

"Can you meet me at Finley's?"

"Sure. Are you okay?"

"I'm fine and leaving now so I'll see you in a few." Sara hung up and raced for the door.

She was out of breath as she got to the bar and sat down. After ordering a martini for herself and a Jack and cola for Chloe, she waited. Chloe finally appeared next to her.

"Hey, you hung up before you told me what's going on." Chloe hung her jacket on the back of the bar stool.

"Here, I got you a drink."

"Okay, this must be good." Chloe giggled as she took the drink from Sara.

Sara held up her glass. "You told me to do it and I did. I sent my screenplay to Peter Harper." Sara sat smiling at Chloe.

"And?"

"He likes it and wants to meet with me." Sara clicked her glass to Chloe's and took a sip.

Chloe set her drink on the bar and almost knocked Sara off her stool as she hugged her. "Oh, my God, Sara, this is huge." Chloe shook her head as she sat back down.

"I know, right?" Sara beamed.

"So, when are you meeting him?"

"I'm not sure yet. I'm waiting for him to answer."

"Shouldn't you be checking your phone?"

Sara pulled her phone from her pocket. "I have been. Nothing yet." She placed the phone on the bar. They both sat staring at it.

"I'm so proud of you, Sara. You've come a long way in these past months."

"I think that was more survival instinct than anything." Tears welled in her eyes.

Chloe handed her a cocktail napkin. "Now, none of that," she scolded. "This is your time and you need to make the most of it."

"Thank you, Chloe, for always being here for me." Sara smiled as she wiped the tears from her eyes.

"That's what a BFF's for, silly. Now, I think this calls for another round, don't you?"

"Absolutely."

"Are you going to tell Lisa?" Chloe asked as she waved for the bartender.

"No."

"Okay." Chloe turned back to look at Sara. "You've never told her anything, right? I mean, about you know who."

"No. Not about that and not about sending the file to Peter."

"Look, Sara, I know you don't feel for Lisa what I think she feels for you. But I think if you really don't think this is going anywhere, you need to break it off."

"I know, but I don't want to hurt her."

"You will either way. Don't you think it's better to do it sooner rather than later?"

"I know you're right and I know she's not the one for me. Maybe there's no one for me."

"Hey, I didn't say that." Chloe took Sara's hand. "I'm saying that maybe you need to concentrate on you and what you want. If this works out for you with Peter and your screenplay, it's going to be a whole new world that will need all your attention."

"You have high hopes for me, don't you, Chloe?"

"Damn right I do and so should you." Chloe slapped her hand on the bar.

"Okay, I'll talk to Lisa, which I really don't want to do, and I'll wait to see what happens with Peter and go from there."

"That's my girl. Check your phone. Let's see if he answered."

Sara picked it up and looked. "Nothing yet...you don't think he's doing this because of her, do you?"

"Because of Claire? Look, Sara, sometimes it's who you know, not what you know, and if this is a result of you knowing Claire, who cares? If it gets you in the door, don't worry."

"You're right. I mean, knowing her wouldn't help if my writing was crap, so maybe I have a shot."

"Of course you do. He'll contact you and you'll set up a meeting and go from there."

"Thank you for having faith in me." Sara lifted her glass.

"Someone has to. You sure as shit don't have any in yourself." Chloe laughed. "We still have to work on that."

"Yes, we sure do." Sara smiled.

Gail Newman

Chapter Thirty-four

THREE DAYS LATER, SARA sat in Peter Harper's office. She looked around the room at the books that lined the shelves and the awards that were placed between them. Stacks of papers lined a small table to the side of a conference table. The dark, wooden desk held framed pictures of actors and actresses she recognized and others of people she assumed were family or friends. She felt a small bead of sweat run down her back as she tried to calm herself. Finally, the door opened, and Peter entered the office.

"Hello, Sara," he said, extending his hand.

"It's nice to see you." She stood to shake his hand.

"Let's sit at the table. I've had your screenplay printed out so we can discuss things."

They settled next to each other at the table. Peter turned his chair slightly toward Sara, the screenplay in front of him. "I was delighted to hear from you, and I apologize for not being able to get back to you right away, but I was on location in Germany."

"There's no need to apologize. I'm sure you're very busy. I'm sorry if I'm taking valuable time away from you."

"Not at all. I was excited to read your work. You may not remember, but I said when I met you that I thought there was something about you that told me I would like your work."

"I do remember that, but I never thought for a moment...so, you liked it?"

"Yes. I liked it very much." Peter smiled at her. "I think there is some work that needs to be done to improve it, but nothing I don't think you can't handle with some help."

"Wow." Sara sat back in her chair, her eyes wide and a hand over her mouth.

"I'm sure you realize that in this line of work, most projects don't make it to the large or small screen. But I think, if you do the work that needs to be done, this screenplay might have the potential to be picked up as a spec script. You need a good screenwriter-slash-producer like me to help you along."

Sara's head was spinning. *This is going too fast. What's the catch?*

"There is one thing," he said.

Here it comes. She closed her eyes for a moment.

"I'd like another writer named Ben Sawyer to help you. He won't be taking any credit should this sell, that will just be you and me. But with his help and my help we may be able to get this onto the big screen. You are going to need to go back and develop some of the characters a little more and tighten up the plot. It's loose in some areas."

Sara sat in silence for a moment. "You're not kidding about this are you?" she asked in a whisper.

"Oh, Sara. You'll find I kid about a lot of things but not about this." He took her hand. "I really think you have a career in this."

"I don't know what to say," Sara said as she looked down.

"Say yes and we'll get started."

She looked up and into Peter's eyes. She was met with a warm smile of assurance. "Yes."

"Wonderful. I'll call Ben and give him your number. He'll have a copy of this before the end of the day and will start making his notes and suggestions, as will I. The three of us will talk on the phone and send emails to discuss our changes. Once a week we'll meet or have a video call to see where we are in the process. Sound good?"

"It all sounds great, Peter. I really don't know what to say except, thank you for giving me this chance. It means the world to me."

"You're welcome, Sara. Now, I can't promise it's going to be easy, and you may not like some of our suggestions, but we'll hash it all out." He walked her to the door and extended his hand.

Not able to contain herself, she hugged him. "Thank you, Peter."

He smiled at her. "It's my pleasure."

Once on the street, she had her phone in hand and already calling. "I did it, Chloe. He's going to help me get this done." She laughed as she listened to Chloe screaming.

***

The next day, Ben called to introduce himself and suggested they meet for coffee so they could put faces with the names. Sara liked him right away. He was a little chubby, with dark hair and a beard, and a bright smile. He reminded her of a teddy bear.

They laughed and chatted, and Sara knew he would be someone that would be in her life for a long time. When she told him she was a lesbian, he laughed and said that was great because they were going to get intimate with their writing and he was happy not to have to worry that she thought he was coming on to her.

Sara left the coffee shop and hailed a cab. She knew she couldn't put things off any longer and called Lisa and asked if she could come over.

"Hi, babe," Lisa said as she opened the door.

"Hi," Sara said as she brushed past her into the apartment.

Lisa stopped her with a kiss. "I'm glad you called. I'm sorry I've been so busy at school."

"That's fine. I understand." The lump in her throat was growing. "Listen, can we sit and talk a minute?"

"Sure," Lisa said, a look of concern on her face. They walked over and sat on the couch. "Are you alright?"

Small beads of sweat formed on Sara's face. "I'm fine. Really."

"Why don't I get you some water?" Lisa started to get up and Sara grabbed her arm.

"No, Lisa. I'm okay. Just let me talk, alright?"

Lisa sat down next to Sara and Sara took her hand. "Look, Lisa, I really like you, but...I'm not ready for a relationship. Not the kind of relationship I think you want or deserve."

"I see." Lisa's voice cracked.

"I think there might be more feelings on your part than there are on mine, and I don't think that mine will change. I don't want to go on and hurt you anymore then I might have already—"

Lisa stopped her, holding up a hand. "Sara, I think I've known from the start that there was something keeping you from me. Maybe you know what it is or maybe you don't. You're right. I think my feelings are more than yours. I guess I hoped yours would change, but I don't want either one of us to be unhappy. This does hurt, but I understand. And I appreciate your being honest with me."

Sara started to cry as she hugged Lisa. "I'm so sorry, Lisa. I really am."

"It's all right." Lisa stood up and put her hand out to Sara.

Sara allowed Lisa to pull her up and they walked silently to the door.

"I hope you find what you're looking for, Sara," Lisa said as she opened the door.

"I hope you do too." Sara turned and left.

Gail Newman

Chapter Thirty-five

"YOU'RE KILLING ME, BEN, you know that?" Sara laid her head on the table. She and Ben were in her apartment working on the screenplay. It was a warm, mid-September day and the breeze was blowing from the open windows.

"Hey, if we make this change I think we're there." Ben stood next to an open window gazing out at the street below.

"I think I've compromised enough." She lifted her head and looked at him.

"I think if you allow this change it makes the story work better." Ben turned to face her. "Look, we've been over this a hundred times. I know it's not what you want, but if you think about it, don't you think this way is more relatable to an audience? Peter has sent this back to us three times now."

Sara held her head in her hands as she said, "Okay."

"Great. I'm telling you this is going to make the whole thing." Ben sat down and began typing.

Sara got up and went to the window he had vacated. Looking out, she briefly allowed herself to think back to where she was a year ago. She didn't allow herself to go back to that time very often. The outcome had been too painful.

She caught glimpses of Claire in the paper or in magazines. Claire won a major film award for the last film that Sara had been with her on. Chloe occasionally mentioned things about her in passing or she would point out Abby standing in the background of a picture, but Sara refused to express any interest in what she was saying. Her days and nights were now consumed with work at the bookstore and writing.

"Sara?"

"Sorry. Did you say something?" She came back from her reverie.

Ben was getting up from the table. "I said that I made the change and wanted you to take a look before I send it off to Peter."

"No, that's fine. I'm okay with it. You can go ahead and send it."

He sat back down and after a couple of clicks he announced,

"Alright, there she goes."

Sara walked over and touched his shoulder. "Thank you, Ben. I couldn't have done it without you."

"No, you did it, Sara. You just needed a sidekick to help make it better. Hey, let's go get a drink to celebrate."

That was the last thing Sara felt like doing. For some reason, she wanted to sit and cry. *Maybe I need to release whatever this is I feel inside.* She decided not to let it get the best of her. "Come on, let's go. I'm buying." She smiled.

Later that evening, when she was home alone, she allowed herself to cry until she couldn't anymore.

* * *

Sara and Ben spent time over the next several weeks with Peter, fine-tuning the screenplay. During one of their meetings, Peter outlined what the next step would be.

"Sara, all you have to do is talk up your work at these networking events." He sat across from her as Ben paced nearby. "I'll be with you for as many as I can."

"'As many as you can.' What does that mean?"

"It means that the three of us will be at some, you and Ben will be at some, and some you may have to do some alone." Peter took her hand. "You've got something really good here, Sara. We just have to go out and sell it."

"Okay, I get it. I may not like it, but I get it."

Peter nodded his head. "Yes. You do know, and I think that once you start talking to people about your work, you might surprise yourself. It's you and your screenplay and you are there to tell people about it."

Gee, sounds like something I've heard before. 'Just an event with a friend.' Great. I know how that turned out.

CHAPTER Thirty-six

OVER THE COURSE OF the next few weeks, Sara, Peter, and Ben made the rounds to different events that Peter arranged for them to attend both in California and New York. For each event, Peter briefed Sara about who would be attending and he also went over some of the talking points so Sara could get a feel for what to expect.

Peter made the introductions and started the conversations. Sara pushed herself to engage whomever she met and worked on her approach. When Peter was unavailable, she attended the events with Ben. She relied on Ben to introduce her to people she didn't know while she made sure to greet those she did. Peter's words stuck in her head. "You never know who is going to be interested. You have to get out there and meet and greet. It's all about timing."

Back in New York, Sara sat alone in the backseat of the car driving her to the evening's event. Peter and Ben were both unavailable. Peter assured her there would be plenty of people she knew who would be happy to introduce her around.

This networking event was at a private home. Sara looked out the window as the car pulled up in front of a townhouse, lights shining brightly from the windows. As she got out of the car, she took a few deep breaths to calm herself. *It's okay,* she thought as she walked up the steps to the front door and rang the doorbell. Sara was delighted to see Evelyn, a woman she had met at a previous event and enjoyed speaking with, open the door.

"Hello, Sara. Won't you come in?" Evelyn smiled warmly.

"Hello, Evelyn. It's so nice to see you."

"Let me have your coat. I'm sure you know some of the people here and I'll introduce you to anyone I think you should meet. Peter speaks very highly of you and is working hard to get your screenplay sold."

"I think highly of him as well." Sara smiled.

"I really enjoyed reading your screenplay," Evelyn said as she returned to Sara after hanging up her coat.

"Really?"

"Yes. I thought the story was moving and the characters well-formed. I think you'll enjoy meeting some of the people who are here tonight. I'm sure someone will be interested enough in your screenplay to see it come to fruition."

Sara chuckled. "I appreciate your wishful thinking."

Evelyn linked her arm through Sara's. "Let's get started by getting you a drink and then I'll introduce you around. I might be quick with some people as they are not people who can help you. If it's someone I think you should speak to, I'll mention the screenplay. You know, pique their interest. Then we'll move on. If they're interested, they will seek you out later or I'll point you back in their direction so you can talk more."

"Sounds like a plan."

After getting Sara a glass of wine, Evelyn took her around the room and made the introductions. As Sara circled back to get another glass of wine, she took a closer look at the people in the room. It dawned on her that most of them were women. She didn't have a chance to think about it further before Evelyn was back at her side.

"I think it's going well, don't you?"

"Yes, I guess so. Evelyn is there a reason most of the people here are women?" Sara thought better of what she said. "I'm sorry. I didn't mean anything by that. It's just that most of the people at the events I've attended with Peter were men in suits with more of a business feeling."

"The women here tonight either own or work for production companies that produce all types of films, whether it's indie or mainstream. They are who you need to meet to get your work sold. These are some of the most powerful and influential women in the business. The reason it doesn't feel like a business meeting or a networking event is because these are my friends. We come together to talk and share ideas and have some wine. I invited you because, after reading your screenplay, I thought that these are the people you need to meet."

"Wow, thank you."

"Don't thank me yet." Evelyn nudged Sara's shoulder. "Grab your wine and let's get back to it."

They approached three women standing together. Evelyn made the introductions and then told them that she had read Sara's work and thought it was a project someone should really get behind. Sara was peppered with questions about the plot and about her own ideas on how it should come to fruition. Sara was cautious at first. Peter had told her not to say too much about what she thought the direction of the project should be in order not to scare off any potential backers who might think she wanted too much control. She carefully chose her words, offering different ways she thought the project could be accomplished.

The discussion went on for about ten minutes with Evelyn ending the conversation with the promise that she would make sure the three had copies of the screenplay the next morning. Walking away, Evelyn again linked her arm through Sara's.

"That went well." She smiled at Sara.

"It did. You're amazing, Evelyn."

"You just have to know how to work the crowd to make things happen. In this case, you wrote a fabulous screenplay and I intend to see it picked up. Now, if you'll excuse me for a minute I need to check on things in the kitchen."

"No problem. I'm going to take a short break from all this talking and find the bathroom."

"Down the hall, second door on the right," Evelyn said as she patted Sara's arm.

Sara found the bathroom and gently knocked on the door before turning the knob and stepping inside. She looked at herself in the mirror while she was washing her hands. Chloe had taught her how to apply the right amount of make-up based on what type of event she was attending. And, to Chloe's delight, she had updated her wardrobe. She smiled at her reflection. *Guess I'm right where I'm supposed to be.* She dried her hands, opened the door, stepped out, and walked right into a woman standing in the hallway.

"I'm so sorry."

"Hello, Sara."

Sara was momentarily stunned. "Hello, Abby."

"I thought I saw you when I came in. You look well." Abby gave Sara the once over.

"Thank you. I am well."

"There you are, Abby," Evelyn called from down the hallway.

"I'll be there in a minute," Abby called back.

Sara saw her chance to make her escape. "Good to see you, Abby," she said as she rushed past her.

Back in the living room, Sara stopped for a moment and scanned the room. *What do I do? If Abby is here, is Claire here too? Oh hell, who cares if she is? Calm down, pull up your big girl panties, and do what you came here to do—sell the screenplay. But if she is here, I'll need another drink.*

She walked to the bar area, got another glass of wine, and joined the group of women Evelyn was speaking to. She was listening to their conversation when Abby came and stood next to Evelyn.

"It's about time she finally got here." Evelyn laughed as she put her arm around Abby. The other women in the group also laughed as they exchanged greetings with Abby. "Abby, you know Sara, don't you?"

"Yes, I do."

"You know she has written a fabulous screenplay that we are working to get sold."

"Yes, I do."

I don't want you to know anything about me. Oh God, please don't let my face show what I'm thinking.

"Sara, I think I told everyone here about your screenplay after I read it." Evelyn smiled warmly at her. "I think it's quite good."

"Thank you. I appreciate your support."

"Ladies, if any of you would like a copy, let me know and I'll make sure you receive one."

The subject changed, and Sara excused herself from the crowd. She decided she would leave as soon as she could. She went to the bar to return her wine glass, chatting with some of the other women as she went.

As she turned to look for Evelyn to thank her for the evening, Abby made her way over to her. "No need to rush out, Claire's not going to be here."

"I'm not rushing anywhere."

"Good, then let's talk a moment." Abby motioned toward the hallway as she walked away.

Sara hesitated before following her into what appeared to be Evelyn's office.

"Glad to see you're doing well," Abby said as she leaned against the desk.

"Are you now, Abby?"

"Yes, I am. Why wouldn't I?"

"I don't know, maybe because you never liked me."

"Don't be ridiculous. Of course I did." Abby gave a wave of her hand.

"Well, you could have fooled me."

"Look, I don't have to explain my past behavior to you. I have a job to do and that's to look out for Claire's best interests."

"And somehow I got in the way of that?"

"I have no intention of explaining to you my relationship with Claire."

"Then why did you want to talk to me?"

"I wanted to tell you that I didn't approve of the way Claire handled the situation with you."

"Okay. Is that all?"

"No. I also think you should have given her a chance to explain."

"Are you kidding me?" Sara's voice started to rise but she quickly realized where she was. She lowered her voice. "She broke my heart as she played some sort of game with me and all the while she was carrying on with someone else."

Abby walked over and stood directly in front of Sara. "You have no idea what you're talking about and if you had given her the chance to explain, you would know that." She walked past Sara to the door and turned back to her. "Her heart was broken too."

Sara stood there. She felt tears welling up in her eyes. Taking a few deep breaths, she composed herself. Back in the living room, she thanked Evelyn for the evening and left.

Gail Newman

Chapter Thirty-seven

A FEW WEEKS LATER, as Sara was leaving the bookstore, her phone rang. "Hello, Peter."

"Hello, Sara. Where are you?"

"I'm just leaving work."

"Is there any chance you might be able to come to my office?"

"Of course. I can grab a cab and be at your office in fifteen minutes if that will work?"

"That will be perfect. See you in a few."

He hung up before Sara could ask why he wanted to see her. When she arrived, she was greeted by his assistant who showed her right into Peter's office. She was surprised to see Ben there as well.

"Sara." Peter greeted her with a kiss on the cheek. "Come and sit here."

"What's going on?" she said, eyeing them suspiciously.

Peter pulled up a chair and sat next to her and Ben stood next to Peter. "We sold your screenplay."

"I'm sorry, what?"

"We sold your screenplay," Peter repeated.

"I don't think I understand." Sara shook her head.

Peter and Ben looked at each other. "I think she's in shock," Ben said with a laugh.

Peter took her hand. "The night you went to Evelyn's and met the ladies there..."

"Yes." Sara nodded.

"Some of the ladies own their own production company and want to buy your screenplay."

"Are you kidding me?" Sara jumped up out of her chair.

"Not only do they want to buy it, they want you to work on it with them," Ben added.

"Wait. You're sure they don't want to take it on an option and have someone else rewrite it?" Sara asked as she walked across the room and then back to sit down in her chair.

"No. And that doesn't happen very often." Peter took her hand and held it.

"I can't believe this. I don't know what to say." She stood up, pulling Peter with her and hugging him. Next, she grabbed Ben and hugged him.

Peter walked to his desk and hit the intercom. "You can bring it in now."

Seconds later the door opened, and Peter's assistant brought in a bottle of champagne and three glasses and set them on the table. Peter opened the bottle and poured them each a glass.

"A toast," he said as he smiled and held up his glass. "To Sara. I knew when I met her good things would happen for her."

Sara started to cry. "I don't know what to say except thank you. Circumstances in my life led me to meeting you, going home, throwing out that old screenplay I told you about, and starting this one. And to you Ben, for allowing me to write what I wanted but all along nudging me to write it the way it needed to be written. I will forever be grateful to you both." Holding up her glass they clicked them together and each took a sip. She set her glass on the table and wiped the tears from her eyes.

"So, what is the name of the company?" she asked as she sat and retrieved her champagne glass.

"It's called ELA Productions," Peter answered.

"ELA? Is that someone's name?"

"It's the abbreviations for the partners in the company. As we go forward with scheduling meetings for production and casting and directing, you will get to meet them. They would like to start having some of those meetings next week. You're going to be very busy, Sara. I think it's time to quit your day job."

"Never in a million years did I think I would hear those words." Sara grinned.

"Everything is being written up. Our first meeting will be to go over the financials. Things like what their offer is to you and whether you accept it. From there, we'll think about the cost of production."

"I don't know anything about that," Sara said, waving her hand.

"That's what my company does for you," Peter said. "We'll work through all that with you. If you don't have your own attorney or financial consultant, we can help you with that as well. We'll give you some names and set you up to meet them."

"Do I need all that?" Sara asked.

"It's best if you do. That way you can keep your personal finances separate from what we are doing for you and from what ELA is doing."

Ben put his arm around her. "There's going to be a lot of people coming into your life now, Sara, and Peter and I will do our best to help you get through it and learn as you go."

"That's right. ELA will probably want to make some changes in the writing and Ben will still be with you on that. It's going to be a process and I can't promise all of it will be easy, but if all goes well I think we'll all be happy with the outcome."

"I seriously need to wake up from this dream." Sara started to cry again as she held her arms out to Peter and Ben for an embrace.

She called Chloe from a cab and gave her the news. As the cab pulled up in front of her apartment building, Chloe greeted her with two bottles of champagne so they could toast the night away.

Gail Newman

Chapter Thirty-eight

THE NEXT DAY, SARA quit her job at the bookstore. She also met an attorney Peter recommended, as well as a financial advisor. After meeting with each of them, she felt ready for the first production meeting which Peter had scheduled for the following week at ELA Production offices.

Sara occupied the days leading up to the meeting with long walks, drinks with Chloe, and treating herself to a massage and facial, something she had never experienced before. She thoroughly enjoyed both and promised herself to have more in the future.

When she arrived for the meeting, she found Peter and Ben waiting in the lobby for her. They made their way up to the eleventh floor and were shown into a conference room.

"Take a deep breath, Sara," Ben whispered in her ear as he pulled a chair out for her.

"Never mind breathing," she whispered back. "Can you hear my heart pounding?"

"Not to worry." Peter smiled at her. "While you've never done this before, we have."

Sara heard voices in the hall, and then the door opened. Three men and two women arrived, pads and pens in hand. Sara learned that they were part of the staff at ELA and would be taking notes and providing information as the discussion ensued. She was also told that they were awaiting the arrival of the head of ELA. A moment later, the door opened and in walked Evelyn.

"Hello, all," she said as she entered.

Sara's mouth dropped open.

"Hello, Evelyn." Peter greeted her with a kiss on the cheek.

"Peter, my dear, so good to see you. You too, Ben," she said as she shook Ben's hand.

Sara rose from her chair as Evelyn approached her.

"Hello, Sara." She smiled warmly as she greeted Sara.

"Evelyn, I had no idea." Sara struggled to get the words out.

"That this is my company?" She looked at Peter. "You didn't tell her?"

"I decided it would be better to wait until we had the meeting."

"Well, I don't know why, but here we are. Let's all sit down, shall we?" Evelyn sat in the chair at the head of the table. "Sara, come sit next to me."

Sara moved to the chair next to Evelyn.

"I'm sorry you were caught off guard, Sara. I wasn't kidding you when I told you that I really liked the screenplay. In the days after our get together, I met with some of the ladies that were also there. Some of them had a lot of interest in it. There were those who wanted to option it and have it rewritten by someone else. There were those who wanted to buy it outright. Well, after those discussions I thought, what the hell? Why should I let someone else's company get it when I like it so much? So I contacted Peter, and here we are."

Sara listened carefully, but when Evelyn stopped speaking, she had to remind herself it wasn't a dream. *Say something.* "Evelyn, I am thrilled that you liked it, but to have you want to make it into a movie is beyond my wildest dreams." Sara's voice choked with emotion.

Evelyn patted her hand. "I can tell you one thing. You're going to be quite busy with this project and with what I foresee happening for you when it's done. I think you're going to find that you will have offers to adapt some projects that are coming up, and hopefully, we'll get to see you write another original screenplay. You're very talented."

"Thank you." Sara smiled as the tears ran down her face.

Evelyn pulled a box of tissues from somewhere under the table.

"Now, dry those eyes. We have work to do," she said as she dabbed the tears on Sara's face.

Peter cleared his throat. "Shall we get started?"

Location costs were discussed. Sara had written the screenplay to take place in London. It was decided that filming would take place there. The production start date would be decided once a director and cast were chosen. Peter would arrange where auditions would be held.

"Sara, I would, of course, like to have your input on these decisions, but ultimately the final decisions will be up to ELA to make," Evelyn said as she walked with Sara to see them out.

"I understand, Evelyn, and I'm sure I'll have plenty of questions for you as we go forward."

"I'll be seeing you again very soon."

"Evelyn, thank you again. I really can't believe any of this."

"No need to thank me. As I said, I think you're very talented. Now, give me a hug and I'll see you next time."

Sara smiled as she hugged Evelyn. She walked quietly with Peter and Ben until they got in the elevator, where she yelled "Oh my God" as the doors were closing.

Gail Newman

Chapter Thirty-nine

CHLOE LOUNGED ON THE bed drinking a glass of wine while Sara packed. "Let me get this straight. You still haven't cast the two main characters?"

"Correct. Derrick had someone he wanted to see here, but she had already left to go out of the country. She'll be in London, so we will see her when we get there. The other lead can't do it due to a scheduling conflict, so we've had a setback."

"Suppose you get someone with an English accent."

"You're joking right?" Sara asked as she folded a pair of pants and placed them in the suitcase. "You know that actors can change their accents. That's why they're called actors."

"Oh, yeah, guess it's the wine talking."

"I wish you were going with me." Sara sat down on the bed next to her.

"Me too. I'm sorry, but this photoshoot is a big deal for me. If they like the work I do, I might be able to be one of their regular make-up artists."

"I told you that I asked if you could work on my project."

"I know you did, and I appreciate that, but you know they have who they want."

"No. That still hasn't been decided on." Sara got up and returned to folding clothes.

"I find that it's best not to get my hopes up. Besides, when you become a big wig you can insist that I do the work." Chloe climbed off of the bed. "What time is the car coming to take you to the airport?"

"Should be here in about half an hour."

"Okay. I'm going to grab a cab and go home. I want you to call me as soon as you arrive."

"I will," Sara said with a laugh.

They walked arm in arm to the door.

"Remember to stand your ground," Chloe said as she hugged Sara.

"I will. And when I call you, I'll tell you every detail." Sara returned the hug.

Chloe opened the door. "I'm really proud of you, Sara."

"Thank you. I couldn't ask for a better friend."

"See ya." Chloe pulled the door shut.

Smiling, Sara leaned against the door for a moment before racing back to the bedroom to finish packing. Half an hour later, she saw the car pull up. She grabbed her suitcase, looked around the apartment, took a deep breath, and went out the door.

The flight was uneventful and she slept most of the way. Before she knew it, she was in a car on the way from the airport to the hotel. Just before the car pulled up in front of the hotel where she was staying, it passed the hotel where she stayed with Claire on their last trip. She felt a slight tug on her heart and quickly brushed it aside.

Chapter Forty

SITTING AT A LONG table inside the studio, Sara sat through a production meeting as Evelyn, Peter, and members of both their staffs discussed logistics with the director, Derrick Owen, who was well known in the business for his technique. Sara listened intently as he explained his vision for the project.

The day seemed endless as they went through the breakdown of the script and discussed how long filming would take so the budget could be finalized. They also discussed the best ways to get the crew to locations to shoot scenes. It was more than Sara had thought about. *I don't see how this is going to happen.*

Late that evening, she was back in her hotel room ready to pass out. Derrick had asked that she join him for dinner, but she politely declined. She ordered room service, took a hot bath, and fell asleep.

***

"Alright, everyone," Derrick said as he handed out bios of the people they were considering casting. "I'm very excited for you to see one actress in particular, but, unfortunately, she won't be able to get here until a little later this afternoon. In the meantime, we will be looking at some of the actors and actresses that are auditioning for the supporting roles."

"I hope they're better than the actors we saw in New York," Evelyn said as she shook her head.

"Now, Evelyn, be nice," Derrick said.

"I am nice. I just don't have time to listen to anyone whom I don't think will fit." Evelyn turned and smiled at Sara.

Sara couldn't help but smile back and nod. She had seen first-hand the way Evelyn dismissed those she didn't deem right for the part. She gave them just enough time to get a few lines out before shouting "Next." Those she thought might be worthy were allowed to finish the sample lines and then she questioned them. "No sense in allowing them to go on when they're not right for the part," she had told Sara after she noticed Sara's startled reaction the first time she shouted "Next" during an audition.

After lunch, they continued seeing people. When Sara thought she couldn't take anymore and hoped they would call it a day, Derrick announced that the actress he had been waiting for had arrived. Since he had refused to tell anyone who it was, whispers spread around the room. He exited the room and came back with a stunning woman.

"Everyone," Derrick said. "Not that she needs any introduction, but may I introduce Claudine Monet."

The room erupted in applause. For Sara, it was all in slow motion. Evelyn was saying something she couldn't hear, people were moving about, and the next thing she knew, Derrick was walking towards her with Claudine. Evelyn greeted her, and then turned to Sara. Sara stood up.

"Sara, this is Claudine Monet," Derrick said. "Claudine, Sara wrote this wonderful screenplay that we are all here for."

"Hello. It's a pleasure to meet you." Claudine smiled as she extended her hand to Sara.

It's her. Oh my god, it's her. Sara felt like she was paralyzed. She didn't know what to do. She wanted to scream at her and tell her how she had ruined her life, that she had loved Claire, and did she know what a fool she had been made because of it? Did they laugh together during their Thursday nights at the Cameron? *No. I can't do that, but I can get the hell out of here.* Barely getting the words out, she returned the greeting and the handshake.

"Evelyn, I'm not feeling well, and I think I might faint. Can you please get me out of here?" she whispered.

"Claudine, Sara is a little under the weather. Forgive us but I need to take her back to the hotel."

They moved quickly, leaving Claudine, Derrick, and everyone else behind. Peter caught up with them and Sara heard him ask what was wrong. Evelyn asked him to get her car. Once they were seated in the back of the car, Evelyn handed Sara a bottle of water.

"Sara are you alright?" Evelyn asked as she placed her hand on Sara's forehead.

"I'm sorry, Evelyn. The room got awfully warm all of a sudden and I needed to leave."

"Are you sure that's all it is?"

Sara wanted to tell Evelyn everything but thought the better of it. *I don't know whether I want to cry or scream. Better just calm down.* "If it's okay with you, Evelyn, I'd like to reserve comment on that for now. I think I just need to get back to my room and get some rest."

"That's fine. If you need anything, please call me. Otherwise, I'll call you in the morning to check on you."

Evelyn held her hand until they arrived at the hotel. Promising Evelyn she would call if she needed her, Sara got out of the car and made her way up to her room. She lay down on the bed and fell asleep.

When she woke up an hour later, she got up and walked to the window. Her first thought was to call Chloe, but it was the middle of the night in New York and she wasn't sure she was ready to talk yet. *I'll call her when it's morning there.*

Gazing out at the early evening sky, she decided she needed some air to shake off the day. She thought a walk would help her figure out how she was going to handle the situation. She checked her phone and saw there was a text from Peter asking if she was okay. He was at the airport waiting to fly back to New York and would be back in a couple of days. She texted back that she was fine.

She grabbed her jacket and set out first along the river in front of the hotel, and then down the side streets. Glancing in the windows of the storefronts as she passed them, she found herself looking into one that was familiar. It held the candle she had been drawn to when she was in London with Claire. Stepping back, she looked up at the sign and the building. It was the same pub.

She carefully pushed open the door. As if she was in a fantasy, she saw the same table where she sat. Everything was as she remembered. She smiled to herself as she made her way to the table. After she took off her jacket, she sat down and looked around. "I can't believe it's the same place."

"Someone will be right with you," a man called from behind the bar.

"I'm coming, I'm coming," a woman said as she came out the kitchen door.

"Petula?" Sara asked as the woman came toward her.

"Well, looky who came back. So, tell me love, are you still invisible?"

"I did some work on that." Sara laughed.

"Glad to hear that." Petula looked closely at Sara. "Ah, but you've had your heart broken I can see."

"What? No," Sara said waving her hand. *This woman is some sort of a mind reader.*

"Hmm, we'll talk about that when I get back. Let me get you a glass of wine." Petula went to the bar and returned with a glass of red wine.

"Now tell me all about it," she said as she threw the dish towel over her shoulder.

"Okay, you might be right. While working on not being invisible, I might have gotten hurt, but I'm over it now."

"Really?" Petula eyed her suspiciously.

"Yes, I am. I'm here for work and starting a new chapter in my life."

"Okay." Petula nodded her head.

"I am."

"Order up," a man yelled from the kitchen door.

"Hold your horses," Petula yelled back. She patted Sara's arm. "I'll be back in a flash."

Sara relaxed and sipped her drink. She watched as Petula brought out a plate of food and walked to the side of the room where the booths were located. Seconds later, Petula came back around carrying the plate of food.

"I don't know why we always have to go through this," she was saying as she passed Sara on her way back into the kitchen.

"Well, I don't know why either, but we do," A woman following her said.

Sara looked up as the woman continued her rant.

"If you would just do it right—" She stopped in her tracks in front of Sara.

"Sara," She said, almost in a whisper.

"Claire."

Petula's return stopped them from saying anything else. She looked at the two of them. "Why both of my favorite birds are here tonight. And if I'm not mistaken, both are suffering from broken hearts."

"Before you make any more of your assumptions, why don't you go and check on my food and bring me another glass of wine?" Claire said pointing towards the kitchen.

"Why don't I just go and do that?" Petula said as she walked off.

"Sara."

"Yes. It's me." Sara steeled herself.

Petula returned and handed a glass of wine to Claire. "Do you two know each other?"

"We've met," Sara answered.

"Why don't you join her?" Petula prodded Claire.

"I don't think I'm invited."

"That would be fine, Claire. Please." Sara gestured toward the empty chair.

"Alright," Claire pulled the chair out and sat down.

"I'll give you two some time." Petula tapped the table and left.

They sat in silence for a moment.

"You look well, Sara. What brings you to London?" Claire took a sip from her glass.

"I'm here for work. My screenplay sold and I'm here for production meetings."

"That's wonderful. Is it the screenplay that we talked about?"

"No. I threw that one out and wrote a new one." Sara folded her arms across her chest as she looked at Claire.

"I see. Are you working with anyone I know?"

"Yes. Peter Harper is helping me through the process."

"I'm so happy for you." Claire smiled. "I don't suppose you'd like to tell me about the plot?"

"No. I don't think I'm ready to share that." Sara reached for her glass.

"Not with anyone or just not with me?" Claire tilted her head.

"I would answer with you, Claire. While I've moved on with my life, that part still stings a little, shall we say."

"Fair enough. I wish you would let me explain." Claire's hand moved toward the middle of the table as if she were reaching for Sara's hand.

Sara almost let down the guard she was so bravely holding up. "What brings you to London?"

"I needed a little getaway. Some time for myself."

Isn't that the same reason she told me as to why she was spending time at the Cameron when she was meeting Claudine? Claudine? Sara began to shake her head.

"What is it, Sara?" Claire looked at her, concern in her eyes.

"Wow. So, I guess I'm still playing the fool. You're here because she's here and she had the nerve to show up today at the auditions. That makes sense now."

"Sara, what are you talking about?"

Sara lowered her voice and said through gritted teeth, "You and Claudine Monet, that's what."

"What?" Claire's voice rose. "Are you kidding?"

"No. I'm not kidding. I know it was Claudine you were waiting for on those Thursday nights and when she stood you up you called me for company. What happened? Did she stand you up so much that you had to move on to me?"

"Sara, darling, you need to listen to me." Claire started to stand up.

"I don't have to listen to anything from you." Sara got up, almost knocking the chair over as she did. "I need to get out of here."

Claire grabbed her by the arm. "Sara, listen to me. I don't even know Claudine. My god, I think I met her once at a premier. I wasn't meeting her or anyone else. I was, it was a plan I came up with that was just…" Claire began to cry.

Sara steadied herself and looked Claire in the eye. "I don't think I can believe anything you say." She grabbed her jacket and left.

Chapter Forty-one

SARA SAT ON THE floor of her hotel room picking at her breakfast and talking on the phone with Chloe. "So, what do you think?" She asked while she stabbed at the eggs on her plate.

"I'm still trying to process the whole thing. I mean, first Claudine shows up, then you meet Claire. That's quite a coincidence."

"I know, right? It just doesn't make any sense. Why else would Claire be here if not to be with Claudine?

"I guess. The strange thing is that Claire said she didn't know Claudine and thinks she only met her once."

"What are you saying?" Sara put down her fork.

"Maybe Claire wasn't meeting Claudine. Maybe I was wrong about that."

Sara took the phone away from her ear, looked at it, and put it back. "Maybe you were wrong?"

"Maybe. I mean we never had real proof."

"What about the card on the flowers? The note I found that looked like a 'C' on it?"

"Okay. There is that. I'm wondering why Claire would say she didn't know her."

A knock at the door stopped Sara from answering the question. "Chloe, I have to go. I think Evelyn is here. She called this morning to check on me and said she was going to come up. I'll call you later."

"Okay. Talk to you later."

Sara struggled to get up from the floor, stretching her legs out as she did. *Remember not to sit on the floor so long.*

"Good morning, dear." Evelyn smiled brightly as she greeted Sara.

"Good morning, Evelyn. Please come in." Sara gestured toward the room.

"This is lovely," Evelyn said surveying the room. "Are you feeling better?"

"Yes. Much better. I'm not quite sure what got into me."

"Really?"

"Yes. I think the day was just a little long."

Evelyn walked to the sofa and sat down. "Come sit with me and let's talk about that." Evelyn patted the cushion next to her.

Sara obliged and sat down.

"I could go about this in a roundabout way and go through the motions and ask why you suddenly felt ill, but I'm not that kind of person." Evelyn shook her head. "So, I'll cut right to the chase. You reacted to seeing Claudine."

Sara was shocked. "Evelyn..."

"It's quite alright, dear. I know all about it. We girls run in tight circles."

Sara put her hand up. "Evelyn, I don't think you know or understand."

Evelyn took Sara's hand and held it. "Ah, but I do know. It's you, my dear, who doesn't understand. Let me explain without giving away anyone's secrets. God knows they're theirs to tell." Evelyn laughed. "I got a call last night from someone who knows I'm here with you and was concerned about you and wanted my help. I knew all I needed to know and that's why I'm here. Sara, I want you to listen to me carefully." Evelyn grew serious. "There never has been, and never will be, anything between Claire and Claudine. They don't know each other, and honestly, I don't think they've ever met."

Sara tightened her lips as she tried to stop the tears. "Evelyn," she whispered as she lowered her head. "You know this for sure?"

Evelyn gently tipped Sara's face up with her finger and looked at her. "I promise you."

Sara sat and took it all in. "Then why all the theatrics?"

"That my dear, you'll have to find out for yourself if you're interested." Evelyn picked up her purse. She opened it, removed an envelope, and handed it to Sara as she stood up. "This was delivered to me this morning. Now, I'm going to give you a few minutes to get yourself together. I'll be downstairs in the car waiting. We have a lot to do today. You have nothing to lose by getting the answers to your questions." She smiled at Sara, turned and left.

Sara stared at the envelope. Her first thought was to rip it up. After taking a few calming breaths, she slowly opened it and began to read the letter tucked inside.

Sara,

My darling, once again it seems I've made a mess of things. I've wanted to tell you everything, and when we met last night, I thought I might finally have the chance. But things didn't go as I'd hoped. I leave for New York tomorrow. I'll be at the pub tonight if you'd like to come and give me a chance to set things straight, if for no other reason than to just let me explain. If you're not interested, I'll understand, and we'll just leave things the way they are.

Claire

Sara put the note back in the envelope. She sat for a moment before gathering up her things and leaving to join Evelyn.

***

Evelyn briefed Sara in the car about what happened after they had left the previous day. Derrick let Claudine run through the lines and thought she would be perfect for the role. Evelyn also explained that since she had bought the screenplay, it would be up to her and her team to ultimately decide on the actors that were cast for the parts. Sara was there as the writer to help with writing any changes in the screenplay.

Once they were at the studio, Sara watched more auditions while her mind kept going back over Claire's note. She was still unsure what to do as they sat in the car on the way back to the hotel. When she got to her room, she decided to call Chloe even though it was late and updated her on what happened.

"What do you think you want to do?" Chloe asked.

"I think I owe it to myself to go and hear what she has to say. It would be nice to think I wasn't being made a fool of. Plus, I'm not the same person I was then. I can handle anything she has to tell me and walk away."

"Don't you feel anything for her anymore?"

"Those feelings were based on something that wasn't real. I'm still not sure what she was doing but I'm going to go and find out once and for all," Sara said, trying to convince herself as well as Chloe.

"I think that's the best thing to do. Once and for all get it all out there in the open."

"I'll let you know what happens."

Gail Newman

Chapter Forty-two

SARA WALKED THROUGH THE streets until she found herself standing in front of the pub. She hesitated a moment before pushing the door open. She stood just inside the door until Petula came out from the kitchen. Smiling, Petula pointed toward the booths.

Sara found Claire sitting in a booth facing her. Not a word was spoken as Sara took off her jacket and sat down. Nothing was on the table except Claire's glass of wine and a small vase with flowers in it.

Petula came around and placed a glass of wine in front of Sara. "Let me know if you need anything else." She smiled at them and walked away.

"Thank you for coming."

Sara picked up her glass and took a sip of the wine. "Do me a favor, Claire. Just tell me the truth." She set the glass on the table.

"Of course." Claire nodded. "Let me begin by saying how sorry I am for all this. I didn't go about things the way I should have. I'm sure you'll have some questions. Please ask them. I want to make sure you understand. I was attracted to you from the moment we met, but with my career just starting, I couldn't get involved in any type of relationship. I didn't know what types of relationships you had previously or might be interested in. So, you became my assistant and we began there. As my career took off, I was guided by people who thought it best if I kept my personal preferences in romantic partners to myself."

"Basically, you're trying to tell me you were a lesbian all along?" Sara took a sip of her wine.

"Yes."

"I find that hard to believe. What about Michael? I thought he broke your heart?"

"Sara, I must ask that you promise that anything I tell you remains private. I mean, I know you're not very fond of me right now, and if you choose, you can say anything you want about me to the press and I'll deal with the consequences. But anything I say about anyone else you must keep to yourself."

"I'm only here for my truth, Claire. I'll keep anything else to myself. I promise."

"Thank you. Michael is gay, and our so-called relationship was a cover for him, for both of us. It ended not as a lover's quarrel but because he didn't hold up his end of the bargain. We were great friends and were both going to come out publicly, but he got cold feet and that ended our friendship. Of course, the press thought it was the end of our romantic relationship."

"What about all the nights he stayed over and how you cried over the break-up?"

"Ah, those nights. We had the best times staying up and gossiping. That's what best girlfriends do. No one does it better than a gay man." Claire laughed before becoming serious again. "When he decided he wasn't going to come out, he also decided that it was best for us not to be friends. That's what I cried over."

"That makes no sense. Why couldn't you stay friends?"

"Because if I were to come out, the press would have looked at him and he couldn't deal with that."

"Okay, so that explains you and Michael." Sara finished her wine. "Now about Claudine."

Claire picked up her glass and took a long sip. Petula appeared out of nowhere and placed two more glasses on the table and hurried away. Sara watched her go. "At some point, you also need to tell me about her."

"Yes, there's a story there." Claire smiled. "Alright, about Claudine. As I said, I don't know Claudine. I may have met her once. You could explain to me though, darling, wherever did you get that idea?"

"Well, there were some things that were going on that might have led to that assumption. Remember when I found the red bra in your hotel room?"

"Yes."

"I didn't think it was anything you would wear but another woman might. I overheard you on the phone saying you could still smell perfume that was lingering on you after a rendezvous. You played that song repeatedly at the townhouse. You know the eighties song "Usual Place." It's about a woman. Then you were staying at the Cameron and well, I was with Chloe, and we were trying to put things together, and Chloe read an article that Claudine was staying at the Cameron. I had no idea who she was until Chloe told me she was a beautiful French lesbian and that seemed to add up to what was going on."

"But you never asked me." Claire ran her hand over the tabletop.

"No. I thought that if you trusted me, you would tell me."

"Fair enough. I should have trusted you enough to tell you everything without trying to orchestrate how I thought things should happen. I will now. I wanted you to think that I could be interested in a woman and, knowing you had a previous relationship with a woman, that if you were interested, you might feel more comfortable approaching me if I gave you some hints. I didn't think my hints were working, so I took them to the next level, which was letting you think I was seeing a woman. I sent flowers to myself—"

Sara stopped her. "Wait. I saw the card on the flowers and it was signed Claude."

Claire sat for a moment. "Oh dear, that's right. No wonder you thought it was Claudine. No darling, the Claude on my card was Claude Debussy from 'Claire de Lune.' The song I told you I was named after."

"Are you kidding me?" Sara's voice rose.

"Why would I kid you? Especially now?" Claire tapped at the table with her finger.

"Wow." Sara wrapped both hands around her wine glass. "I also found a note in your nightstand that you were writing. It began with a "C" and you were writing about misjudging feelings and a second chance."

"So, you went through my nightstand." Claire smiled knowingly.

Sara's face turned red. "I was concerned that you hadn't come home, and I thought I was trying to help you."

"That was an 'S' and the note was for you. I was having doubts about how I was handling things and was going to come clean and tell you everything."

"But you didn't," Sara countered.

"No."

"Another thing." Sara tapped on her glass. "What was with the whole cell phone thing and who were you talking to if it wasn't Claudine?"

"Ah, yes. That's another thing I need to explain." Claire squirmed in her seat. "That was Abby."

"Abby?" Sara's eyes widened.

"Yes. Most of the time I was talking to Abby. If she wasn't available, I pretended to be talking to someone when I knew you were in the house, so you might overhear."

"Abby, who hates me, was in on this the whole time?"

"Darling, Abby doesn't hate you. In fact, she is not very happy with me about this at all."

"I find that hard to believe," Sara said shaking her head.

"It's true. I have to tell you something about Abby and this is something I'm going to have to ask you to keep to yourself."

"Okay, this I have to hear. I promise not to say anything." Sara made a little cross over her heart.

"Abby is also a lesbian and we were together before my career started. She became my agent when we realized we made better friends."

Sara sat back in the booth taking it all in and then leaned forward. "I can't believe it."

"It's true." Claire took a sip of her wine and continued. "She has always liked you but has always been a little jealous. Well, not jealous. Protective. She might have been a little harsh on you since she knew of my feelings for you and is always looking out for me. I can tell you that she was not happy with my plan and said I should have been upfront with you from the start."

"This is crazy. I wouldn't have guessed about Abby. I never got the lesbian vibe from her."

"She's just so busy being bossy it doesn't come across." Claire smiled. "But she's in a long-term relationship and is very happy."

"Get out of here. She's with someone?"

"Yes. And I guess that's another thing I need to tell you." Claire picked up her glass and downed the contents. She had no sooner put the empty glass on the table when Petula appeared with two more glasses and a plate of cheese. She disappeared just as fast.

Sara was amazed. She looked at Claire. "Seriously, before I leave here tonight you have to tell me about that woman. Sorry. Back to Abby."

Claire took a piece of the cheese and ate it before continuing. "Abby is Evelyn's partner."

"I'm sorry?" Sara sat straight up.

"Abby and Evelyn have been together for about fifteen years. That's how Evelyn knew what was going on and how I was able to get that note to you this morning."

"So that's what she meant when she said that about running in tight circles." Sara sat silent for a moment. "Wait a minute, did she buy my screenplay because of you? Because if that's the reason I want nothing to do with it." She started to stand up.

"No, Sara. Please sit down."

Sara sat down.

"I had no idea. Abby had been keeping tabs on you and would let me know what you were up to. When Peter started to market your screenplay, she was able to get a copy. She really liked it and gave it to Evelyn to read. They arranged to have the party so that you could meet people who would be interested. Once Evelyn saw that there was real interest, she decided that since she liked it so much, she would buy it rather than letting someone else get it. I found out after it all took place."

Sara sat silently for a moment. "Why on earth would Abby be keeping tabs on me?"

Claire took a deep breath. "She knew how upset I was over everything that happened and how worried I was about your well-being. She thought there might be some way she could fix the situation, and by knowing what you were up to, she might be able to do something. She's a fixer. She also thought you had a lot of potential, so when she found out you had contacted Peter, she made sure that your work would be looked at and given a chance if it deserved one."

Sara put her head in her hand and then looked at Claire. "Isn't that kind of what I said before, that they did this for you?"

"No, no, no," Claire said. "Believe me, Evelyn makes very solid business decisions. If she didn't like your work, she would have passed on it without considering what anyone's feelings were."

"What about Abby? She couldn't influence Evelyn?"

"Not in Evelyn's business. While ELA might mean Evelyn Loves Abby, Abby does not have a say in it other than recommending actors she might see fit for a part. That's her job as an agent."

Sara couldn't help but smile. "That's what the company letters stand for?"

"They are quite a pair, those two." Claire smiled back. "Even after all these years, they love each other very deeply."

Sara nodded thoughtfully as she glanced around the restaurant.

"This place has a calming effect," she said as she picked up a piece of cheese. "How did you find it?"

Claire looked around. "It was my first trip to London. I was auditioning for a small part in a film. I was terrible, the film was terrible and when I left the audition I wandered around the streets not really paying attention to where I was. I was lost in thought about what I was going to do if I were terrible at acting. When I stopped to see where I was, I saw this little candle in the window and it just drew me in."

"That's what happened to me," Sara said, almost in a whisper.

"I wandered in and there was Petula. She took one look at me, told me what she was going to bring me to eat, and then proceeded to somehow know what I had been through and how I was going to be a big success. I thought she was trying to be nice and cheer me up but what she said to me that night really made me think about what I wanted in life and I decided to go out and get it. I come here every time I'm in London. When I come, she always seems to know what's been going on in my life and how I'm feeling. I really believe she's psychic. Although she always gives me a hard time about my food."

They sat quietly for a few minutes.

"Is there anything else you'd like to ask me?"

"I'm not sure, Claire. That was a lot to take in."

"Yes, I guess it was. May I ask you a question?"

Sara crossed her arms and leaned on the table. "You can ask but I may reserve my right to answer."

"Fair enough." Claire nodded. "Are you seeing anyone?"

Sara thought for a moment about how she should answer. *I have nothing to hide.* "I was seeing Lisa, the dentist I told you about."

"You're not seeing her anymore?"

"No. We were together for a few months. She wanted more than I was able to give her."

"I see."

"Do you, Claire? Do you see how what you did to me ruined everything?" Sara asked as her eyes searched Claire's face for an answer.

"I know that I hurt you deeply, and for that I will be forever sorry. I should have taken my chances and allowed us the opportunity for things to happen naturally. I was afraid that you might find someone else, just as I was that night I saw that redhead hitting on you."

"What are you talking about?"

"That night at Todd's party. That little redhead would have been all over you if I hadn't sent Abby over." Claire tapped her finger on the table.

"Is that why she came and got me?" Sara thought back to that night.

"Yes, and good thing too."

"Wow. Look, Claire, I was already on to her and had no interest, so nothing was going to happen. That said, now that I think about it, she might have been a little hard to get away from." Sara chuckled.

"From my vantage point, I could see her zero right in on you. I was not going to let her get in my way."

"And there we have it, Claire. What? Get in the way of your plan. It was all about your plan."

"Yes."

"Yes, and that's why we are where we are." Sara shook her head.

"And where is that?" Claire lowered her eyes.

"Sitting here, finally getting it all out in the open. Were you ever going to tell me the truth? Did you ever think about how I would react when I found out? Everything happens for a reason, Claire. You broke my heart and it allowed me to wake up and not be invisible anymore. It allowed me to write and look what happened—I sold my screenplay. That wouldn't have happened if I'd stayed in your plan. I would have gone along with it until you told me, and maybe then I wouldn't have been strong enough to recover. But I did, and I'm not the same person I was. My eyes are open, and I want them to stay that way. I want to see what's ahead of me, with work, with love, with life. That wouldn't have happened if you hadn't broken my heart. I guess for me, that was what had to happen." Sara saw Claire crying and handed her the napkin from under her glass.

"Well," Claire said as she dabbed her eyes, "I guess this is all for the best." She sat for a moment and looked at Sara before getting up from the table and standing next to her. She reached down and took Sara's hand. "I love you very much," she said as she looked into Sara's eyes.

"I know."

Claire released her hand and left without another word. Sara sat there for a few moments and finished her wine.

Petula came around to the table. "You alright, love?"

"I honestly don't know. I did what I came to do, which was end something that, to me, wasn't real. But I don't feel the way I thought I would."

"And how was that?" Petula sat down and looked at Sara.

"I guess I thought it would be relieving or freeing, but somehow I feel lost." Sara leaned forward towards Petula. "Like I lost something that was real."

Petula reached her hands across the table and Sara placed her hands in them. "I believe, very much, that all those feelings were real. I think it was the way the feelings were handled that was the problem.

Perhaps if you take those feelings and allow them to be front and center, you'll be able to get what it is you're looking for."

Sara smiled at Petula, squeezing her hands as she did. "I think I need to move here just so I can see you all the time."

"Come on now, love, give us a hug." Petula got up from the table and opened her arms.

Sara warmly returned the embrace. "Thank you for everything," she said as she held on tight.

Chapter Forty-three

"YOU'RE TAKING QUITE A gamble here," Evelyn said, tapping a pencil on the table.

"I know. But at this point, what I have got to lose?" Sara stared at the door, willing it to open. She took a deep breath when Derrick stepped through it.

"Good morning, ladies. How are we this morning?"

"Derrick, dear, we've had a little change of plans," Evelyn said.

"What now, Evelyn? Have you decided about something that's just going to ruin the perfectly good morning I was having?" He set his paperwork on the table with a thump.

Evelyn smiled at Sara. "Now why in heaven's name would I do a thing like that? Why don't you get yourself a cup of coffee and sit down? We have a few more minutes."

"What are we waiting for?" Derrick asked as he poured coffee into a cup.

"Sara decided to try something she thought might give the project a boost. I'm helping and now we're waiting to see if the fruits of our efforts will produce anything."

"Alright, I'm game. Shall we all just sit here and look at the door?" He joined them at the table.

"For now," Sara said.

They sat silently as the moments passed. Just as Sara was about to give up, she heard footsteps in the hall. She looked at Evelyn who smiled back. Abby opened the door and held it open for Claire.

"I'll have you know that my client was supposed to be catching a flight this morning," Abby told them as they continued into the room.

Evelyn smiled. "Why, Abby, my darling, so happy to see you're in a good mood."

Abby shot Evelyn a look. "I'll have you know I'm in a perfectly wonderful mood this morning."

Derrick, taken by surprise, scrambled to his feet. "Why, ladies, this is just so unexpected. I had no idea you were coming."

"Oh, don't get all mushy, Derrick. This is a business meeting." Abby rolled her eyes in his direction.

"Derrick, dear, sit down and let me handle this." Evelyn pointed toward his chair. She rose up from the table and greeted Claire, kissing her on both cheeks. "Claire, thank you so much for coming this morning."

"I have to admit, Evelyn." Claire looked directly at Sara. "It was quite a surprise to get your call."

"Thank you for coming," Sara said, holding Claire's gaze.

"My pleasure."

"Alright, let's get on to with it. Claire can make a later flight if she decides to." Abby walked to the table and pulled out a chair for Claire and then one for herself. "From what I understand, you want Claire for one of the lead roles in this project."

"Yes, we do," Evelyn said.

"Oh my God," Derrick gushed.

Evelyn turned toward him. "Derrick, please keep your comments and emotions in check."

Derrick nodded as he sat back in his chair.

"I've read this script, but Claire hasn't. She only knows the brief description I gave her this morning and, of course, what you told her last night, Evelyn. I think it's best if she has a chance to read it before making any decisions. This role is different. This character is different from any she's played before. Quite frankly, we worry about what this type of role could do to her career," Abby said as she clasped her hands together.

"We understand that, and we are perfectly willing to let Claire read it before she decides. We're just very happy, Claire, that you were willing to meet with us."

"I'll be happy to read it and see if it's something I'd be interested in. May I ask if you have cast the other lead?" Claire said.

Evelyn looked at Sara and Sara gave her a slight nod.

"We were thinking of Claudine Monet," Evelyn said, clearing her throat once she got the words out.

"Claudine, how interesting." Claire smiled as she raised a finger to her lips and gently tapped them.

"Yes. We thought the pairing of the two of you would bring definite interest to the project. Of course, Claire, the decision is entirely up to you." Evelyn shuffled the papers in front of her. "Should you decide to come aboard, we'll discuss everything else."

"I'm sorry, we need to keep this short. I think we know all we need to know unless you have something else for us. We'll consider this project very carefully," Abby said as she looked around. "Claire will decide if she is leaving today—"

Claire interrupted her by raising her hand in the air. "Abby, I won't be leaving today. Evelyn, give me a day or two to read the script and I'll let you know whether or not I'm interested."

"That sounds wonderful, Claire. Take your time. Do you have any questions for any of us while we're all here?" Evelyn asked.

Claire looked at Sara for a long moment. "No. I think I have everything I need for now. Abby has the script, so I'll get to it and let you know." Claire pushed her chair out and stood up.

Following her lead, Abby stood up. "Alright, as Claire said, we'll let you know."

Evelyn got up and kissed them goodbye. Sara watched as Derrick approached them and muttered something to each of them. Sara made her way around the table and extended her hand to Abby.

"Thank you, Abby," she said as she shook Abby's hand. She turned to Claire. "Thank you so much, Claire, for taking the time to consider this." She extended her hand to Claire.

"It is my pleasure." Claire smiled as she took Sara's hand and held it for a moment before she and Abby left.

Sara returned to her chair and sat down. Evelyn sat on the corner of the table and looked at her. "What do you think?"

"I have no idea."

The next day and a half were spent in continuous meetings. Not a word was spoken regarding the meeting with Claire and Abby. Evelyn had warned Derrick that if he breathed a word of it to anyone, she would make sure he had no breath left in him.

Sara busied herself in the evening, walking along the riverfront. She decided to stay away from the pub for the time being. She spoke to Chloe, but was careful to leave the meeting out of the conversation. *The fewer people that know, the better.*

Late in the afternoon of the second day, Evelyn told Sara and Derrick that Abby had called. Claire still hadn't made a decision. Evelyn had prearranged a private meeting room at the hotel for one o'clock each of the next two days in hopes they could meet there once Claire decided. Evelyn added that it was an appropriate time to start drinking if things didn't go the way they hoped.

It took a little detective work, but Sara was able to find out the alias

Claire was using while staying at the hotel. She found a private room in the studio and called the hotel. When she asked for "Ms. Austen" she was put through to the room. After a few rings, Claire answered.

"Claire, it's Sara. I was wondering if you would like to have dinner with me this evening. I thought maybe I could answer any questions you might have."

"I'd like that. If you're sure?"

"Yes. I think it might give you better insight into the character." Sara looked around to make sure no one was coming into the room.

"Then of course. Where shall we meet?"

"I'll send a car to your hotel to pick you up. Say seven thirty?"

"I'll be ready. Is there anything else I need to know?"

"No, not really."

"I'll see you later."

Sara hung the phone up and took a deep breath.

Chapter Forty-four

AT SEVEN FORTY-FIVE the doorbell rang. Sara looked around one more time before going to answer it. She opened the door to find Claire looking stunning in a light blue double-breasted pantsuit. Her blonde hair fell softly to her shoulders.

"Claire, please come in. You look lovely." Sara gestured towards the room.

Claire walked in and turned to Sara. "Thank you. I must admit I was a little surprised when the car brought me here."

"Come and have a seat. Can I get you a glass of wine?"

Claire walked to the sofa and sat down. "Yes, that would be nice. Are we leaving to go somewhere for dinner?" Claire asked as she adjusted the large accent pillow behind her.

Sara opened a bottle of wine that was chilling in a cooler. "No, I thought this environment might be a little less public for our discussion. I'm having dinner brought in. It should be here in a few minutes." She poured the wine and handed a glass to Claire as she sat down beside her. "Thank you for coming."

Claire leaned forward and gently touched her glass to Sara's. "To your project," she said as she settled back on the pillow.

"I understand that you're still undecided. I thought that maybe, having this conversation would help you have a better understanding of the characters." Sara took a sip of wine.

"I must say I am intrigued by the plot. I sense that you changed direction along the way."

"Why would you think that?"

"I've read enough scripts in my career. I can tell when the writer has had a plot set from beginning to end. Those are usually the ones I pass on. The ones where I think the writer has changed their minds as they write the character or the plot are the ones I find most interesting. I like to find out why those changes were made."

"So, you have finished reading it?"

"Yes, I have." Claire took a sip of wine and placed the glass on the table in front of the sofa.

The doorbell rang before Sara could say anything else. "Excuse me. That will be dinner. Let's save this conversation until later." She greeted the two waiters as they pushed the cart into the room and set the plates on the table.

"Shall we eat?" she asked Claire after the servers left.

"That would be lovely." Claire rose from the sofa and walked to the table. Sara pulled a chair out for her. "Thank you."

Sara brought the wine bottle to the table and refilled both their glasses before sitting down as well.

Turning her attention to the plate before her, Claire smiled. "What do we have here?"

Sara placed her napkin on her lap before answering. "It's beef bourguignon. I hope you like it."

"This is delicious," Claire said after tasting it.

"I'm glad." Sara smiled as she, too, tasted the food.

They ate in silence for a few minutes until Claire looked at Sara. "I have to say beef bourguignon is my favorite meal and this is by far the best I have ever tasted. Was this prepared by the chef in this hotel? Because if it was, I'll be staying here from now on."

Sara reached for her glass of wine and took a sip. "It was prepared elsewhere, and I had it brought in."

"Well, you simply must tell me where it's from," Claire said as she waved her hand at the serving tray.

"If you must know, Petula made it for us."

"Petula? Are you telling me that Petula from the pub made this?"

"Yes, I am." Sara nodded.

"My God, that woman is full of surprises." Claire laughed. "But then, so are you. I told you about my love for this dish, didn't I?"

"You did."

They looked at each other for a moment and then quietly continued with the meal.

Once they were done, Sara said, "If you're finished, would you like to continue our conversation about the script?"

"Of course. That's what we're here for."

"Perfect. Why don't we take our wine and go back to the sofa?"

Claire took her wine glass as Sara grabbed the bottle from the chiller.

"Might as well get what you must be wondering about out of the way," Sara said once they were settled on the sofa.

"And what do you think that is?"

"Oh, come on, Claire. You know it's about Claudine."

"I wasn't wondering about that at all. Why, she's perfect for that role." Claire smiled as she ran her hand through her hair. "I was wondering why you wanted me."

Sara thought for a moment and looked at Claire. "I guess I'm taking a chance on you."

"My, my. Taking a chance on me. That's interesting." Claire took a sip of wine.

"Yes. I'm taking the chance that you might want to explore what the public reaction would be to your taking this type of role and how it might affect your personal life."

Claire sat silent for a moment. "Are you wondering that, if I take this role, I might offer insight to the public that I'm a lesbian?"

"I wondered how you will answer the questions from the press as to why you decided to take such a role."

"I would answer as I have answered any questions about any of my previous roles. That my decision is based on the character, the plot, and a director I want to work with."

Sara moved closer to Claire. "But why this role in this project?"

"Because I found the character intriguing."

"Intriguing? Interesting. What else?"

"So, you did change the ending, didn't you?" Claire smiled knowingly.

"Yes."

"Let me guess." Claire tapped a finger on her lips "Our heroine was supposed to fly off alone, strong in her belief that she had left the woman who hurt her behind and in the past, and she was going on to a new and better life."

Sara chuckled. "Well, she did hurt our heroine badly and deserved exactly what she got."

"Oh my. I'm afraid to ask what you originally did to her." Claire laughed.

"I did change that a couple of times. Let's see, first she died a painful death, but I couldn't do that. So, then I let her stay alive, hiding from her truth in a miserable marriage to a man."

"And her truth was that she loved a woman and wouldn't admit it." Claire nodded.

"That's right." Sara poured more wine into their glasses.

"And so, *Flight to Paradise* now ends with our heroine and her love on their flight together to start their new life. Why did you change it?"

"I didn't want to. As Ben and I were finishing, he kept harping on me to make the change. He said that anyone interested would want it to end that way, that the audience would want it to end that way. Finally, he appealed to my heart and asked what I really wanted. I had to admit that that was the ending I would have hoped for." Sara looked away as she didn't want to look into Claire's eyes.

"Well, you certainly have given me a lot more to think about." Claire rose from the sofa. "It's getting late and I should be off."

"Of course." Sara jumped up from the couch. "Let me call for the car for you." She picked up the phone. "The manager will be here in a minute to take you down," she said, hanging up the phone.

"Thank you for a wonderful dinner. I think I'll have to get a flat here and hire Petula full time."

There was a knock at the door and Sara looked through the peephole to see who it was. "He's here," she said turning to Claire. "Thank you for coming."

"My pleasure," Claire said walking out the door.

Sara closed the door and leaned her forehead against it.

Chapter Forty-five

SARA WAS HAVING TEA the next morning when Evelyn called. Claire decided to take the part and Evelyn wanted to celebrate by throwing a welcome party for the entire cast that evening. Abby insisted that publicity of Claire accepting the part be delayed until she had a proper news release, so the party would be kept quiet and would be held at the private home of one of Evelyn's friends.

Sara spent the day in production meetings before going back to the hotel to change. Evelyn had arranged for a car to pick her up and bring her to the party. The home was a short drive outside of London and Sara was content to look out the window at the beautiful countryside as it passed by. *I could live here.*

The car turned off the road and up a driveway to a quaint stone house. Sara took a deep breath when she got out, inhaling the fragrant air that greeted her. A butler met her at the door and directed her into a large living room where members of the cast were beginning to gather.

"There you are." Evelyn greeted her with a warm hug and kiss.

"This is lovely," Sara said as she looked around.

"Isn't it? My friend Joan has lived here for around twenty years. I love coming and staying here. I'll introduce you as soon as she comes out of the kitchen. She's just checking on things."

Sara took another look around the room. "I don't see Claire or Abby. They haven't arrived?"

"Not yet. Neither has Claudine. I guess they want to make an entrance." Evelyn laughed, then nudged her gently. "You and I have never had the chance to talk about all these relationships. I know that Claire told you about me and Abby."

"Yes, she did. I have to say I was concerned at first."

"Concerned? Really, dear? Why?" Evelyn asked, her hand on her hip.

"I'm sorry. I don't mean that I was concerned that you and Abby were in a relationship. I think that's wonderful." Sara blushed. "I meant I was concerned about how that relationship and knowing how Abby has

191

felt about me in the past would hinder the project."

"Whatever do you mean?"

"I never thought Abby liked me." Sara shook her head.

Evelyn laughed. "That's not surprising. She is protective of Claire."

"Then I was afraid that your interest in my screenplay might just be a favor for Claire and I didn't want that."

"Let me tell you something about Abby. Yes, she comes off hard, and she is when she must be. But she appreciates talent and she saw talent in you regardless of what your relationship with Claire was. When she brought me the script, she told me I needed to read it and that I needed to produce it. She was right."

"I guess I could use a little more self-confidence."

"You have it in you, and it will grow as you get more work. In fact, I have more work for you. When we're done with this, I have some other projects that we are optioning that I want you to look at. And of course, we're all expecting to see more of your original work in the future."

Sara couldn't help but hug her. "Thank you so much," she said, grinning ear to ear.

Their hug was interrupted by the sound of applause. Sara turned to see Claire and Abby come into the room, followed by Claudine.

"Ah, and here they come now. What did I tell you? Making a grand entrance. Come, let's go prostrate ourselves before them." Evelyn laughed as she linked her arm through Sara's.

After the greetings were made, everyone settled around the living room immersed in different conversations. As the evening continued, Sara made her way around the room, chatting with different people. Occasionally she would glance over her shoulder to look at Claire who was in deep conversation with Abby, Evelyn, and Claudine. Her interest piqued every time she caught a hint of Claire's laughter. Excusing herself from the person she was talking with, she made her way past the four of them on her way to the bar.

"White wine, please," Sara said to the bartender.

"I would like one as well," said a voice from beside her. It was Claudine. "And so, you are the writer of this script?"

"Yes, I am."

"We really haven't had a chance to get to know one another. I would like to get a feel for your script from your point of view. Perhaps you can join me in my room at the hotel?"

Sara felt the blood rushing to her face. *Don't blush, don't blush.* "Maybe it would be better to meet while we are at the studio."

"But we have so much in common. I can tell." Claudine put her hand on Sara's arm.

Sara started to panic. Words tumbled around in her head but nothing came out of her mouth.

"Claudine, there's someone I'd like you to meet. Would you excuse us, Sara?" Abby asked as she took Claudine by the arm and walked away.

"I'll see you later." Claudine smiled at Sara.

Sara breathed a sigh of relief as she took her waiting glass of wine from the bar and looked around the room. She took a big sip and walked toward the open doors that led to the patio. Looking up at the night sky, she took some deep, calming breaths.

"It's a lovely evening, isn't it?"

Sara turned to see Claire walking toward her.

"Yes, it is," Sara said with a smile.

Claire stood next to her and looked up. "I was getting ready to leave and wanted to say goodnight."

"What about Abby and Claudine?"

"They're staying. I've just had enough for the evening." Claire rubbed her arms. The night air was becoming chilly.

"I've had enough too," Sara said as she glanced back inside.

"My car is waiting if you'd like to ride back with me."

"If it's no trouble."

"Your hotel is near mine. It's no trouble at all."

They returned to the living room and said their goodbyes. Sara caught a glimpse of the fuss Claudine made over Claire as she was saying goodbye to Evelyn.

***

Sara and Claire chatted lightly as the car made its way from the house. Sara looked out at the dark night sky and pondered everything that had transpired from when she first met Claire until that moment. Before she knew it, the car pulled up in front of her hotel. Claire was about to say something when Sara cut her off.

"Claire, I need to talk to you about all this," she blurted out.

"All what, my darling?"

"I have to talk to you." Sara looked at Claire.

"Alright." Claire instructed the driver to take them to her hotel. Without a word, they went up to Claire's room.

"Now, what's this all about?" Claire asked as they sat down on the sofa.

"Claire, I can't let you do this movie," Sara said, shaking her head.

"What do you mean?"

"I just can't let you. The scenes you would have to do with Claudine. I mean, I just don't think you can do them."

"The love scenes?"

"Yes, the love scenes. I only had a moment with Claudine tonight and I swear, if you hadn't sent Abby over, she would have been all over me. Her with that French accent."

Claire started to laugh. "First of all, I can handle Claudine. And second, I never sent Abby over to you."

"Didn't you see what was going on?"

"Of course I did, but you're a big girl. I have no reason to save you from another woman. You've made that perfectly clear. So if another woman is interested in you, then it is your decision what you want to happen."

Sara got up and began to pace. "Well, I don't think anyone can handle Claudine, and I don't think that you and she in this movie doing those scenes is a good idea."

"But you wrote those scenes."

"I know. But I didn't write them for you to do with her." Sara waved her hand in the air. "The thought of her touching and kissing you...I can't handle it. It's bad enough that I have those images in my head from when I thought you were with her."

"As we know, that never happened. I was never with her."

"I know, but the images are in my head and I have to get them out." Sara held her head.

Claire took a breath and let it out. "Then I have to ask you this again. Why did you want me to do this movie?"

Sara stopped pacing and looked at Claire. "I said I was taking a chance on you."

"You said it was to see how I would react to public speculation."

"Yes, I know, but I obviously didn't think it all the way through. I wasn't thinking about what would happen when it came to the love scenes or how I would react or what I might want."

Claire got up and walked to Sara and stood in front of her. "Then what is it you want?"

"Oh, to hell with it." Sara looked Claire in the eyes. "I want you."

Claire began to smile. "Really?"

"Yes, really. After all this, and everything I thought, the only thing that is real is, I've always loved you. That is, if you'll still have me?

Claire wrapped her arms around Sara. "I've never wanted anything more," she said and then she kissed her.

As their kiss ended and they held each other, Sara whispered, "You know what else I want?"

"What is that?" Claire asked as she cupped Sara's face in her hand.

"I want to do love scenes with you for the rest of my life."

Gail Newman

Chapter Forty-six

"IF YOU HOLD STILL a minute, I can get this hooked." Sara was struggling to close the back of Claire's dress.

"Oh, bloody hell, I knew I shouldn't have had lunch," Claire said as she wiggled around.

"You said you needed lunch since you wouldn't be eating anything tonight because you are nervous."

"I say that all the time. I didn't expect Petula to make such a delicious lunch that I wouldn't stop eating when I should have."

"There, it's closed. We knew when we hired her as our cook and housekeeper we'd be in trouble." Sara stepped back to look at Claire. "You look beautiful, my love."

"Thank you, my darling, and so do you."

Almost a year had passed. The movie had been completed and it was the opening night premiere in London. Sara and Claire were now splitting their time between New York and a house they had bought just outside of London.

"The car is here," Petula said as she stuck her head inside the bedroom door.

"And, no thanks to you, I barely got in this dress," Claire scolded her.

"It's not my fault you eat everything I put in front of you. God knows how you stay in the shape you do." Petula waved her hand towel at Claire.

"Now, ladies, let's not get into this now." Sara laughed as she held her hand out to Claire. "Let's get you to the car. And get you back down to the kitchen." She pointed to Petula.

"Shall I have something waiting for you when you get home?" Petula asked.

Claire started to say something, but Sara stopped her. "No, thank you. You have a good night and we will see you in the morning."

"Alright then, good night." Petula shut the door behind her.

"You know if I didn't love her so, I really think she could make me go mad." Claire picked her cape up from a chair.

"You two really know how to pluck each other's feathers." Sara shook her head. "She loves you too, you know."

"Yes, aren't I lucky?" Claire mumbled.

"Yes, you are. Let's get going. We can't be late. Abby will have our heads. She has the whole arrival planned." Sara opened the door and they went to the car.

The car slowed and stopped as it neared the theater. One of Abby's assistants would call the driver and let him know when to proceed to the front.

Sara fidgeted with her bracelet. "Aren't you nervous?"

"I'm always a little nervous at these things but I've done enough to know what the routine is."

"I know that. I meant aren't you a little nervous about the premiere?"

Claire took Sara's hand. "All I know is that I am here with the woman I love, who wrote a beautiful screenplay that I am so happy to be a part of."

Sara started to laugh. "I'm always amazed at how good an actress you are."

Claire tilted her head. "What? That was the truth. You'll know when I'm acting."

Seconds later the call came through and the car took them to the theater.

"Ready?" Sara asked, kissing Claire on the cheek.

"Ready." Claire smiled at Sara and took a deep breath as the car door opened.

Voices rose and cameras flashed as they stepped out of the car. Abby appeared out of nowhere and stood next to Claire.

"Alright, it's the usual routine. You do the slow walk up to the 'step and repeat' step and repeat area. Pictures and interviews will take place, and eventually we'll all get inside for the introduction and discussion by Derrick and Evelyn and then viewing of the movie. Do you need anything?"

"No, I think I'm good." Claire turned to Sara. "Are you alright with everything, my darling?"

"Yes. Abby went over everything with me and I know what to do."

"Alright. Let's get this show on the road." Claire straightened her shoulders, flashed a huge smile, and began to walk toward the theater.

Sara trailed slightly behind as the noise and cameras continued to flash. She made her way to the side of the step and repeat area. She heard someone call out her name. Turning, she found herself caught in a huge embrace with Chloe.

"Oh my God, I've missed you," Chloe cried.

"Me too," Sara said as they broke apart and then hugged again.

"I know it hasn't been that long. I mean, I saw you last month but it's not the same as when I'd stop by your apartment or we'd spend Sundays at Finley's." Chloe wiped away her tears.

"Hey, I'll be back next month and we'll be able to pick back up. Plus, you're going to be here for the next week." Sara grabbed Chloe's hand. "And who says you'll have any time for me given your current situation."

"Now, that's a situation I have you to thank for." Chloe laughed. "If I hadn't come to visit, I might not have ever met Claudine and fallen in love."

Sara's eyes opened wide. "I'm sorry, did you say the 'L' word?"

"Let's just say I'm very happy and she is too and hopefully things will continue that way."

"Seriously, Chloe. Have you told her you love her or are you just saying that to me? I've never heard you say that about anyone."

"I'm saying it to you, and if things continue then yes, I'll say it to her. But if things don't work out, only you know and that will be the end of it."

"Ah, Chloe, you are such a hopeless romantic." Sara laughed.

"Okay, so I got the very brief 'stay out of the way' message from Abby, but what's the real deal with all this?"

Sara linked her arm through Chloe's and they made their way closer. "As you can see, Claire and Claudine are being interviewed by different members of the press. Somewhere around here, Evelyn, Derrick, and other cast members are being interviewed. Then they all gather up there at the step and repeat for pictures."

"Of course, that means you too, right?"

"Yes. Abby told me she would come and get me for that."

"So, while we have a few minutes, I loved that interview that Claire did where the reporter asked how she will be able to do any love scenes with men now that we all know she's a lesbian."

Sara smiled. "Her answer was great."

"What was it again." Chloe thought for a moment. "Oh yeah. It was something like, 'Well that's why I'm such a good actress. I've been a lesbian all along and you believed all those scenes.' It still cracks me up."

"There have been some ups and downs since she came out, but for the most part it's all good."

Just then, one of Abby's assistants came to get Sara.

"I'll see you later." Sara gave Chloe a quick hug.

After stopping for a few questions, she found herself standing off to the side of the step. She smiled as she watched Claire pose with Claudine, Evelyn, and Derrick. A moment later she heard her name announced and she strode up and took her place for the pictures. One by one, Evelyn, Derrick, and Claudine hugged her as she made her way until she finally reached Claire.

Claire reached out her hand and Sara took it as she moved to stand next to her. More pictures were taken until they found themselves alone as the others stood off to the side.

A reporter called out, "Sara, are you happy with Claire's performance and your vision turned out?"

"I'm so very proud of the way this project turned out and with the way everyone involved saw it through. There are so many people to thank. Evelyn, whose help and friendship has been such a gift. Claudine and the other members of the cast who so wonderfully embraced the characters. Derrick who held them all together. Peter and Ben who were with me from the start. Thank you all." She looked over at them and smiled. She turned to face Claire. "And to Claire, my beautiful Claire, whom you all know in a few short months will be my wife now that we can get back to wedding planning. Her performance in this film takes my breath away and her portrayal of her character was more than I could have hoped for."

Applause erupted as Sara finished speaking.

Claire's eyes filled with tears as Sara took her hand and lifted it to her lips.

"I love you, my darling," Claire whispered.

"Let's take our flight to paradise," Sara said.

The End

About Author

Gail is a native of Long Island, New York, currently living and working near Virginia Beach. Discovering a long-forgotten manuscript, Gail was excited with the prospect of trying her hand at writing again. Her mind opened to new ideas which culminated in her writing Sunlight in the Shadows.

Excited with new thoughts and ideas, Gail plans to continue writing and sharing her stories.

Gail and wife Elise split their time between Virginia and their second home on Shelter Island which they love to fill with friends and family.

Facebook: GailNewmanFans

Note to Readers:

Thank you for reading a book from Desert Palm Press. We have made every effort to edit this book. However, typos do slip in. If you find an error in the text, please email lee@desertpalmpress.com so the issue can be corrected.

We appreciate you as a reader and want to ensure you enjoy the reading process. We would like you to consider posting a review on your preferred media sites and/or your blog or website.

For more information on upcoming releases, author interviews, contest, giveaways and more, please sign up for our newsletter and visit us as at Desert Palm Press: www.desertpalmpress.com and "Like" us on Facebook: Desert Palm Press.

Bright Blessings